KRISHNA'S MILL

KRISHNA'S MILL

STORIES FROM INDIA

THOMAS K. SHOR

CITY LION
PRESS

To those who told me their stories
I dedicate these

Contents

Krishna's Mill

MAHAYOGI SHIV NATH

I

This is the story of Mahayogi Shiv Nath, the charismatic, self-proclaimed holy man and founder of India's cotton empire known for its flagship factory, Krishna's Mill. The unusual course of Shiv Nath's life, the way he was seemingly singled out from the start with favor, might—even if only for the sake of entering into the spirit of the story—cause the most ardent atheist to suspend his disbelief and entertain the possibility that although he himself might not have been chosen for extraordinary deeds, there might be others who have.

The events recounted here unfold in India. It is important to know that the Hindu god Krishna—one of India's most important gods, often depicted as a mischievous young flute-playing cowherd with a penchant for stealing butter—is to a large swath of the population the highest lord.

It is believed that Krishna weaves this world out of his supreme consciousness, and that we are all being churned, spun, and woven into something we never could have imagined. How different from science's clockwork universe of things governed by cause and effect is the notion that behind it all a god is dreaming this world and all of its actors into existence, and that he does so out of a sense of play. Mad as it might seem in the modern context, this story begs one to be open to the possibility that Mahayogi Shiv Nath's life bears the mark of the intervention of Lord Krishna himself.

It's as simple as this: When Krishna wants to build a temple he faces an immediate problem: being a god, he has no money—and to build a Krishna temple you need money, even if it be a philanthropist's. So Krishna starts weaving. Krishna weaves lives out of the warp and woof of the very stuff of the universe. For him, time is nothing. Patience has no meaning for him since he lives outside time's round. He plants his seeds. He harvests. He plays his flute and people dance to his tune, without quite knowing why.

Because Krishna is a weaver of lives, and mischievous, it was a cotton mill that he conceived, to be called Krishna's Mill. From the extraordinarily good luck he imbued in its proprietor, the subject of our story, as well as our protagonist's innate propensity for things spiritual, both the impulse and the money would, with time, conjoin to build the temple.

Let me make one thing clear: so far there is no temple. This is only my theory. Yet everything seems to be headed that way as if with purpose—as if the temple will, with time, reveal itself as the cause of all that came before it. While this logic might seem backwards, it isn't necessarily, not if what the ancient Indian philosophers said is true when they described this world as *lila*, the divine dance of existence, not fundamentally different than a dream. And who knows? Even physicists now play with the possibility that time's arrow is multi-directional.

Although most of us believe as we pass through our days that we ourselves are writing the script of our life's story as we go along, the truth might very well be that we are like actors on a stage, spontaneously delivering our lines with a passion that weaves its spell not only on those with whom we share the stage, but on ourselves as well. This view holds that we are so mesmerized by our performance in the darkened theater that we cannot see the strings that guide our movements.

This inevitably leads to tremendous confusion and to the many unanswerable questions that hang at the center of so many people's lives. Chief among them: Why do I lead the life I lead and not some other? Why is one man born to be king and another a beggar?

Occasionally a crack forms in the perfectly executed script, and the otherwise hidden hand behind our fates becomes manifest. This is more apt to happen in—or around—people who are called upon to do great deeds. They seem to be guided by fate, by inordinate good luck borne on an almost superhuman confidence—like the great hero who boldly walks across battlefields to save innumerable people as if secure in the knowledge that he cannot be hit.

It was just such a life that has been enjoyed by Mahayogi Shiv Nath.

Back in 1942, Shiv Nath was an eighteen-year-old village boy from the Punjab who came to Bombay with a dream in his head, a few rupees in his pocket, and a dog-eared copy of the book *Think and Grow Rich* under his arm.

Although thousands have streamed into Bombay, India's commercial hub, every day for centuries with dreams of riches, most end up in the ever-growing slums that attract loose human beings torn from their moorings in the countryside like filings to a magnet. Dreams dashed against the reality of cardboard shanties are as numerous as the waves that crash on the beach at Marine Drive, Bombay's famous and fashionable 'String of Pearls.'

What set Shiv Nath apart from the others? Of a million poor villagers that come to Bombay with dreams of riches, perhaps only one creates an empire of the dimensions of his. At its height, Shiv Nath's factories stretched across India's northwest, from Bombay and Poona north to Gujarat.

Back in his home village in the Punjab they had a family guru, a wise man with the gift of seeing past, present, and future. He told the boy's parents when he was only five years old that everything he touched would turn to gold. And thus it was. People wondered at his shear good fortune. He exuded charisma. His luck was so pronounced that even he could not help but wonder whether he was marked out for something. It made him ask the ultimate questions; it compelled him, as he grew older, to turn his attention within and attend to his soul.

Sometime around the age of sixty, he handed his considerable worldly affairs over to his three sons and to his business partner. And as he relinquished control of his factories (many of which were so mired in litigation that it would take the courts years to sort it out) it was with the words, "You do—I pray." And thus, trading in his double-breasted suits tailored in London and Paris for the orange robes of the wandering ascetic, he set off on a pilgrimage to the holy sites of Hindustan. This eventually led him to the Himalayas, where he undertook a life of meditation and vision.

His first pilgrimages were conducted from the back seat of his chauffeur-driven car. When he discovered that his chauffeur was an alcoholic and was selling off parts of the car to finance his habit, even selling the engine for a defective one, the repairs on which he expected his employer to pay, he abandoned such comfort, so unseemly for a wandering holy man, in favor of first-class train tickets and hired cars that would take him to his favorite places of contemplation in the Himalayas.

It was there, in the Himalayas, in a village called Kausani, that I first met Shiv Nath, who had by that time added the appellation *Mahayogi* to his name. Mahayogi is a contraction of *maha* and *yogi*. A *yogi* is a practitioner of Eastern philosophy and mysticism. *Maha* means great. Most know this word from the appellation that was applied to Gandhi, Mahatma—*maha*, great, and *atma*, soul; so when they were calling him Mahatma Gandhi, they were calling him a great soul, an appellation Gandhi resisted being affixed to his name.

Shiv Nath, however, had introduced *himself* as Mahayogi, or Great Yogi, Shiv Nath.

Kausani is most famous for the three weeks that Mahatma Gandhi stayed there in the Himalayan silence in 1929. The place he stayed is now known as the Gandhi Ashram. There is a meditation room and library, a dining hall where one sits on mats on the floor and gets served from buckets of rice, dahl and vegetables. Accommodation is provided in a series of simple rooms available for a nominal fee for people willing to adhere to the rules posted around the grounds, which state that one must follow the principles of nonviolence as set forth by Mahatma Gandhi and not smoke or eat meat on the grounds. It was an ashram without a teacher, presided over by a manager and his minions who all moved around the grounds with a certain shuffle and happy look on their faces as one might see on the faces of inmates in a well-run asylum.

I met the mahayogi almost the moment I climbed the steep stairs and entered the ashram grounds. He came striding toward me, his orange robe flowing gracefully in the gentle breeze, his white hair, well-trimmed beard, and gleaming white teeth all dazzling in the sun's thin-aired brilliance.

"You must be from Scotland," he said, holding out his hand to shake mine Western style. His handshake was confident and strong. "Your sweater is definitely Scottish."

"Actually I am from America," I said, "and the sweater was made in Ecuador."

"Ecuador is also known for its fine wool, isn't it?" He rocked his head Indian fashion, a huge happy smile on his face.

They gave me the room next to his. Though our rooms had separate entrances, they were connected by an old wooden door. The door was sealed shut on both sides and had a large frosted-glass panel. While I couldn't see through the glass panel apart from whether his light was on or off, I could hear much of what went on in his room. That first night I awoke numerous times to hear him turning over in his bed. He didn't grunt or moan as he turned over; rather his bed groaned under his shifting weight as his consciousness emerged from what sounded like a trance-like state. He'd surface, intoning fragments of the ancient Hindu mantras and Sanskrit scriptures he had evidently been reciting in the land behind closed eyes. Then he'd sink back, resume his nocturnal wanderings, and grow silent again.

Mahayogi Shiv Nath took an interest in me and I in him. We became fast friends. And in the week I stayed there we spent much time together. He told me that though most of the time he'd be in his room meditating, I should feel free to come in to continue our spiritual discussions at any time. He asserted that such discussions were of the utmost importance.

The life of a great yogi was obviously a lonely one. "I've not had anyone to discuss these matters with in over ten years," he confessed. "My own family, they think I am crazy. My wife—she died two years ago of a brain tumor—never understood. And my children, they are thoroughly modern, thinking only of money. Their concern *for* me only goes as far as what they can get *from* me. That is the curse of success. All you do is give your children something to fight over. I have shed my responsibilities and now spend most of my time meditating in the Himalayas. When I return to Bombay—it might be after half a year—my children don't even come to see me for two or three weeks. And we live in the same house! If they want to see me it is usually because they want something *from* me, or because of some squabble amongst themselves, always about money, always about affairs of *this* world."

Mahayogi Shiv Nath was not prone to long silences. But after telling me about his family, he was silent. He looked me right in the eye and his eyes became moist. "Even before my wife took ill, I spent most of my time here in the Himalayas. I have a tremendous work to do. The work of yoga is the greatest work a man can do. And I have a destiny to fulfill. The duties of this world have long ago ceased to concern me. Everything comes into existence only to pass away again—except God. We must realize God's manifestation within: then we fulfill what we are here for. This is of paramount importance, before which all else fades. I used to be a man of the world. I stayed in the finest hotels—in London, Paris, Frankfurt, Madrid, in Russia and in Japan. I owned factories and created an empire. But all of that is like nothing—is it not so?"

His smile, so full of innocence and brilliantly white teeth, was impossible to resist.

"When my wife took ill I went back to Bombay, and I stayed there. My wife knew what a sacrifice this was, the disruption of my spiritual practice. She never understood the nature or importance of my inner work; but still, she knew the sacrifice I was making. She said thank you—she actually said thank you." Tears welled up in Shiv Nath's eyes. He took off his glasses and wept. "It was the only time, in our long years of marriage, that she ever said thank you to me."

Mahayogi Shiv Nath wasted no time in telling me about his inner, spiritual life. "I remember quite a few of my previous lives," he told me matter-of-factly. It was the morning after we met. We were sitting outside our rooms on white plastic lawn chairs. Behind us was a broad stone wall, beyond which the land dropped off. In the distance, the high Himalayan peaks were dazzling the distant blue horizon with their jagged pristine whiteness.

He leaned towards me and lowered his voice, his whole being intent on imparting a secret: "I was one of the three wise men of the Christian Bible. We came from the East, following a bright star that had appeared in the sky. The Bible says we brought presents of frankincense, myrrh, and gold to the baby Jesus. This is all true—but entirely incidental.

"Our real purpose was this: we came from the East, you see, and we came to impart the Wisdom of the East upon the boy. We were not Jews, but Eastern sages. You might think this is fantastic, but it is even more fantastic to think that the other two wise men, they are also taking incarnation at this time.

"How do I know this, you ask? You look like you don't believe? We have met, the three of us! It was here, in India. After all those years!

"Which of the three presents did I bring the baby? I told you, the presents were not important. We were actually there to teach the boy, as he grew older. My role was to teach the young Jesus the spiritual and physical practices known as Pranayama, the yoga of the breath, by which one can learn to separate one's consciousness from one's body. He used this technique for the crucifixion. That's why he told his disciples to roll back the rock after three days, for he would be alive. While he was on the cross he practiced the yoga that I taught him, and he let his body die. Once in the crypt, he reconnected his soul and came alive. When his disciples rolled away the rock and he was alive they were frightened. They thought they were seeing a ghost. They thought it was a vision. I know because I was there. Jesus used this to scare them away. I stayed, and by morning we were gone. Jesus and I walked across Persia and what is now Afghanistan to India. It took us seventeen months. Most people don't know this: Jesus lived in Kashmir until he died at the age of eighty-six."

A look of wonder crossed Mahayogi Shiv Nath's face. He rocked his head gently, a wondrous smile of gleaming white teeth spreading, eyes sparkling with both innocence and a certainty that was hard to resist. It was next to impossible not to consider, at least while he spoke, that what he was saying was true.

But he wasn't speaking now; he was looking at me with a sphinx-like smile, rocking his head in wonder. I smiled at the thought of three old codgers, each believing themselves to be incarnations of the wise men, meeting. Only in India.

"Most people, they don't understand these things," he said. "But you—I can tell—you understand the *inner dimensions*."

Mahayogi Shiv Nath had a rich man's paunch. In other places people might display their riches with gold and jewels and slender waists; in India, where many lack proper nutrition, having a large belly commands respect. And Shiv Nath was imperious.

"Gangaaa....Ganga!" Ganga was a boy who worked at the ashram. Shiv Nath would suddenly have the desire for tea or some peanuts, or another blanket because we were sitting outside and he thought I looked cold. He acted as if he expected Ganga to be awaiting his call from around the next corner. And when Ganga didn't appear at once, his majesty's ire would be raised. I then understood that the paunch's command was more than just visual. Shiv Nath would then summon the boy with a roar that could be heard throughout the ashram and to which the boy never failed to respond. He would come running, his hands still dripping from his washing, and present himself before the commanding figure of the mahayogi.

"The boy really loves me," Shiv Nath said. "They all do. They are from the villages. They are very simple people. I am like a father to Ganga. He knows he can go into my room and if there are peanuts or fruit, he can take what he wants."

Every evening Shiv Nath and I would walk beyond the ashram along a dirt road that snaked through the forest. It was a quiet road with open views of the snow peaks. We were often so involved

GANGA & THE MAHAYOGI

in our discussions that by the time we turned around it was already growing dark and we would reach the village in darkness. With one hand on my shoulder and the other on a stick he used as a cane we would wend our way back. And always we were discussing philosophy, like a pair of peripatetic philosophers.

One evening, we were returning to the village in the darkness. Shiv Nath was speaking to me of the spiritual light: "If the sun is in the sky, but the clouds cover it, does not the sun still shine? Or when it is dark here, isn't it light in America? If we put our hand in front of the candle, we are in the darkness. Isn't this true? But the flame is unchanged. Our egos are like that hand in front of the light, like the cloud in the otherwise empty, sun-filled sky. When we are released from the ego the light will shine through us and we will *become* the light.

"We must uncover the light!!"

The moment he said these last words something happened that I have to admit was strange: a glowing light appeared on the wooded slope above the road. Shiv Nath stopped short. He took his hand from my arm, pointed toward the heavens, and though I couldn't really see his face in the gathering darkness, I knew he had a look of sublime understanding. He had the most wonderful smile. "You see," he said, "this is a miracle. We are talking of the light, and a light appears in the darkness. Isn't this wondrous? It materializes out of the darkness. This is tremendous! We are seeing the glow of spiritual understanding!"

"I think it's some sort of glowworm," I said, "Perhaps it's trying to attract a mate."

"There is no mating involved!" he boomed imperiously, his paunch resonating to full effect. "This is clearly the external manifestation of the internal light. It is the light of God. There is definitely no worm involved."

Shiv Nath was used to commanding. If he said the glow needed no earthly source, his word would make it so. He was an alpha male yogi.

Snatching the walking stick out of his hand and leaving

him tottering amid the loose gravel, I scrambled up the slope to the glowing point of light. Gently, I moved the stick under the glowing worm. It was an ugly creature half an inch in length with many sets of stubby legs. I brought it back to Shiv Nath. I made him look at it, expecting the glowing worm on the stick to mark the triumph of rationality over superstition. But it affected him not at all. Nothing could contradict him.

"Isn't this fantastic?" he said. "Look what God has put here for us to see."

Metaphor was for him living reality, and reality had the quality of a dream.

THE MAHAYOGI & THE RISING SUN

One morning I stepped out of my room into the brilliant sunshine. It had rained overnight. The air was crystal clear and the grass seemed greener and to stand up prouder for it. Trees towered overhead, swaying in the gentle breeze. In the distance, plumes of snow like white flags blew from the peak of Nanda Devi and the other high peaks on the border with Tibet. They were visible above an eight-foot high, barbed wire-topped concrete wall, which formed the left-hand boundary of the green area before our doors. The sight of barbed wire and all that concrete always bothered me, marring the view of the eternal heights.

Shiv Nath was sitting on one of the white plastic lawn chairs directly at the base of this concrete wall and facing it. If his eyes were open, surely he could see nothing but concrete, and that at close range. He sat perfectly still, his orange robe played gracefully by the wind. On his head he wore a strange flat square type of headgear.

Approaching, I heard a mantra emanate from him, and I hesitated, realizing he must be in meditation. Like the yogi meditating in the confines of a cave amidst the Himalayan splendor, he sat with his nose to the concrete to keep from distraction.

Since he invited me to disturb his meditation at any time, I drew closer. He heard footsteps, and without turning—or, I suspect, opening his eyes—he knew it was me.

"Thomas," he said, "we must all meditate on the future form of humanity, the form it will take when we are all spiritually transformed." He opened his eyes and looked at me. The contraption on his head was odd, like a flat box of candy wrapped and strapped to the crown of his head with a piece of ocher material tied with a huge bow beneath his chin.

"I am a follower of the great spiritual teacher Sri Aurobindo and his collaborator, the Pondicherry Mother. They taught that just as we evolved from the apes, humanity will evolve further still. Our consciousness will evolve to the point where we don't need these bodies and we will be without birth and without death. We will move through space by thought alone. It is this further evolution of humanity that we must meditate upon; we must call down this spirit of the future; we must participate in this new level of humanity that will bring with it happiness and an end of war and suffering.

"I am also a follower of the ancient Hindu god Bhrigu, through whom I have learned many hidden things—the secret course of my life and the evolution of my soul through my past lives. There is a Bhrigu priest in the Punjab who communi-

MEDITATION ON THE FUTURE OF HUMANITY

cates directly to this god by performing a special ritual. For many years I have gone to him. In fact, it is through him that I learned that I was a spiritual teacher of Jesus Christ, how I was in the Mahabarata, India's great epic, told across the width and breadth of India and as far away as Indonesia by thousands of itinerant storytellers and theater troupes for the past three thousand years. In it is recounted a great war between the Pandavas, or five brothers of the Pandava clan. The Bhrigu priest revealed to me only last year that in a former life I was a great king of that age. I don't tell you this out of a sense of boastfulness or pride, nor to satisfy your idle curiosity. No!"

I asked Shiv Nath how the Bhrigu priest comes to his knowledge of such things.

"The Bhrigu temple contains a huge collection of ancient palm-leaf pages so old that no one knows their age. Upon them is written a script so ancient that only the priest can decipher it. It must be his god that guides him because there are thousands of these ancient pages piled in the Bhrigu temple. Yet he chooses the one on which is written the story of your life: in the tiniest of script it is written in the most minute detail everything that has or will ever happen to you! Isn't it fantastic? Your life, already written! If you go with a particular question he'll find the page that has the specific answer. Whatever you want to know, it is written there. He can tell your future, he can reach far back into your past and describe exactly how it was."

Mahayogi Shiv Nath leaned towards me. "Thomas, I must tell you something of the utmost importance. Fates are intertwined like you cannot imagine: I had a vision last night."

His eyes opened wide, like a child's, bulging beneath his bushy white eyebrows; his head trembled with the gravity of what he was about to impart, the box strapped to his head with its outsized bow under his chin threatening to slide off.

"I saw you in my vision last night, Thomas. You were also in the Mahabarata." He paused to let the gravity of the news sink in. "You were a foot soldier. There was a battle." He raised his arm, swung an imaginary sword, and said as gravely as if it were yesterday, "I saw you get killed."

I truly didn't know what to say, but I didn't have to say a word, for Mahayogi Shiv Nath continued: "One time the priest let me keep the page, which is very unusual. It is that page that I'm wearing on my head. I will show you."

Mahayogi Shiv Nath untied the knot under his chin, releasing the box from his head. He unwrapped it to reveal a wooden picture frame, glass on both sides, sandwiching a piece of paper yellowed with age. The paper, of crumbling palm leaf, was covered with rows of little squiggly marks, undoubtedly the ancient language decipherable only to the Bhrigu priest. Shiv Nath drew my attention to a few scraps of metal foil that clung to one side of the page beneath the glass.

His voice was full of wonder: "For years now I've been meditating on the spirit of the humanity to come, trying to make the new humanity, a *spiritual* humanity, a reality, and in so doing this spirit of the future took on a particular form. You might not believe this, but when the priest pulled this out of the stack, the foil was exactly in the form of the spirit of humanity to come, the object of my daily meditation. I'm afraid it has degenerated with time. I've had this with me for some years now, and I strap it to my head so it covers my crown chakra. It aids my meditation on the future of humanity. It works like a magnifying lens for the higher energies. It is through this meditation that a new humanity will be born. That is why my work is so very important.

"Wait, I will show you what it looked like when I received it." Mahayogi Shiv Nath lifted his corpulence and went to his room, returning a moment later with an envelope inside of which were three photographs. The first was of the page in question before the foil degenerated. It did look like a spirit of some sort, the very likeness of Casper the Ghost standing in a breeze, even with a slit for the eyes. Then he showed me a photograph of the altar at which the Bhrigu priest did his ritual. I had seen many Hindu altars and it looked like one of them, maybe the gods were different, I don't know, but there were an assortment of them in demonic poses inside a glass case, incense smoking before them.

"This was taken before the ritual in which the priest produced this page," he said. Then he triumphantly showed me the third photograph. It was of the same altar, but the head of the main god, right in the middle, was a white glow. "This was taken right after the ritual was over. Look carefully! It is always important for us to look carefully. Bhrigu, right in the middle, is enveloped in a light so bright that you can't even make him out! This photograph captured a miracle!!"

"Did this ritual take place in the afternoon," I asked, "perhaps ending at nightfall?"

"Yes," he answered, a look of wonder on his face. It was clear he was experiencing another miracle. "How did you know?" His voice quavered with emotion.

"That glow around the central figure of Bhrigu," I said, "it is the reflection of your camera's flash."

Nothing could take that look of wonder off Mahayogi Shiv Nath's face.

When I told the mahayogi I would be leaving Kausani, he was distraught. "I have so much more to tell you," he protested. "These are tremendous matters, having to do with fate. Do you know how rare it is to find someone with an understanding of the *inner dimensions?*"

He tried to dissuade me from leaving, but when he saw I wasn't to be swayed from my plans, he had me write down the names of other places of pilgrimage and contemplation in the Himalayas where he could often be found. He also gave me his phone number and address in Bombay, in case fate should find us both there at the same time.

II

Two years later, I was returning to India and flew into Bombay. From the airport I called the number the mahayogi had given me to see if by chance he was in Bombay, and whether I could perhaps stay with him. The mahayogi himself answered the phone. I wasn't sure he would even remember me. When I told him it was Thomas, from Kausani, he was ecstatic.

"This is fantastic," he said, "a miracle that you should call. It was only yesterday I was recalling your name. I meet so many people. But I am old now and forget their names. Yours I have always remembered. Thomas, you must come over at once. Hold on, let me see if my driver is available."

I could hear his feet shuffling across a marble floor, the swish of his ascetic's robes above the hum of an air condition- er. He opened a door and the unmistakable boom of the ma- hayogi's voice called upon a servant to inquire whether the driver was available. Soon he was back on the phone. "Wait at the airport's main entrance," he said excitedly. "My driver will be right there!"

Sitting in the back seat of the mahayogi's chauffeur-driv- en car, we left the airport and passed through what looked like the very gates of Hell—slums and industrial parks of gray buildings greedily spewing forth dark smoke as if to out- do the competition, their effluent pouring directly into brack- ish waterways every bit as horrific as a medieval etching of the River Styx. Then we crossed Muslim neighborhoods and huge chaotic markets, glided by Hindu temples and tall glass office buildings. Finally we were on a road that snaked along the Arabian Sea, waves crashing impressively on the rocks.

The area known as Breach Candy is arguably the finest and most exclusive in the city. That's where we were head- ed. We cut inland a few blocks from the sea and pulled to the curb next to a large white bungalow. It was the only old building in a neighborhood of gated high-rise buildings. It re- tained something of former, perhaps even British, splendor.

There was a gate and a guardhouse, and two men to carry my bags. A third gave me a sharp little salute as I passed. A fourth led me up two flights of stairs and along dark laby- rinthine ways to where a hallway ended at an impressively solid carved wooden door, upon which he gave a short little rap with his knuckle before entering.

It was a huge bedroom with ornate and heavy wooden fur- nishings. The men put my bags down and left me there. From behind another door I heard the distinct sounds of a mahayogi at his toilet. A servant came into the room and proceeded to light incense in front of the outsized, garlanded photo of the Pondicherry Mother, in front of the smaller but equally garlanded photo of the mahayogi's wife, and before a little shrine to Krishna. Before the two photos he lit joss sticks, three at a time, and before the shrine he lit two cones of soft incense that billowed tremendous clouds of acrid smoke. Soon the room was as if a smudged charcoal drawing, everything losing definition in the distance, the far wall eventually merging with the infinite.

Then I heard the toilet flush. The door opened and Mahayogi Shiv Nath emerged, adjusting his ocher robe, his imperious paunch leading the way. Holding out his large hand, we shook hands Western style. He sensed the difficulty I was having breathing. "The incense," he said, "it purifies the atmosphere." My sinuses, which were constricting, thought otherwise.

"You are lucky to find me here in Bombay," he said, a huge grin on his face. "I was in the Himalayas for well over a year when I got a rather desperate call—not more than a week ago—from my daughter-in-law. She is wonderfully intelligent and was able to track me down. She told me that if I didn't come to Bombay immediately my children would start killing each other. She meant it quite literally. It was all about finances, of course. All they know is the affairs of this world, which no longer interest me in the least. They are to be pitied, but also kept from that most heinous of crimes. It was out of a sense of compassion that I have come here. As soon as things stabilize I will return to the mountains and resume my inner work. When I gave up the affairs of this world I left it all to my children and to the man who'd been my business partner from the beginning. I left this bungalow to them all, and they all still live here.

"Many years ago, when I bought this house, I called it Krishna House. It was a house of love. But now it is divided, against itself, like a house possessed by demons. Since none of my sons can get rid of the others, they all still live here, each with their own floor or wing, and they pretend the others don't exist. They have even put lines down the middle of the kitchen and the servants don't even mingle. Each of my sons is afraid to leave this house for fear of giving up his piece of the pie. They prefer to live in misery!"

Just then the door swung open and an early middle-aged man in a dark collarless business suite, his shirt open, came bursting in. He looked like a man who moved freely in the upper crust of Bombay society and would otherwise have been well able to maintain his cool; but it was immediately clear that he was one of the mahayogi's sons when he hurled an angry accusation at his father, delivered with speed and venom in the local tongue.

The mahayogi responded with an equal flash of anger. For a brief moment it was like two male lions meeting, ready to go at each other's necks.

But no sooner had it begun, it was over. The son stormed out. A slammed door left the mahayogi alone with me in the room.

"One of my sons," he said. "Please excuse him, but his mind is deluded by the material world. I must go speak with him." Adjusting his ocher robes, he set out to do the work of this world.

SELF PORTRAIT IN THE MAHAYOGI'S ROOM

For the longest time the mahayogi didn't return. The thickening cloud of incense was like a vice slowly tightening on my head, causing my eyes to smart and tear. So I opened my bag and picked up my book and went into the bathroom, which was large and well apportioned. I found the switch for the fan above the door and propped the door open. I opened the window, hoping I could thus clear the bedroom of its 'purifying' air. I moved a plastic chair that was next to the bathtub to the center of the room so I was in the fan's flow. And there, in exile, I read.

After some time Mahayogi Shiv Nath strode confidently into the bathroom. His face lit up. "Excellent," he exclaimed. "This is most excellent. Very few people would ever think of reading in a bathroom. It shows great intelligence. I also read in here, every morning." And it was true. Every morning at 5:30 a servant came into the bedroom and placed the *Economic Times* newspaper on a little table by the door. The mahayogi would then bring the paper into the bathroom and sit on the toilet for a good half hour, going through the paper's financial pages. There was a large stack of *Economic Times* on the bidet. Interesting reading for a mahayogi.

Perhaps he wanted me to vacate my reading throne so he could, perhaps, vacate his bowels?

"No—no," he said, "it's fine. Please, sit back down. I only came in to see what you were doing. Did you know that there is a different philosophy for every room of the house? My spiritual life began in this very bathroom!"

I didn't know what to say, but since he continued on his own I didn't have to say anything.

"Maybe you don't know this, but when you open your anus," and he made a gesture with his hand like the unfolding petals of a lotus, "when you open you anus and vacate your bowels you create a vacuum, a vacuum that can be filled by a stream of energy from above. An energy current can enter through the crown of your skull and ride down your spine and fill you with tremendous power. This is also true when you urinate.

"I first experienced this over forty years ago. It was during my first visit to London. I stayed in a very fine hotel just off

Hyde Park. In business, one must reach just beyond one's means to embody the imagined future. But that was in my former life, which was all about being external, trying to impress—all of which I am glad to be done with. Anyway, I was sitting in my hotel room when I had the urge to urinate. So I went to the toilet, and as I was urinating this tremendous force, like a flame—a golden force, the most sublime golden glow—descended through my crown chakra at the very top of my skull and descended through my body, infusing every atom with energy. This was in the morning, and later that day I had the very important business meeting I had traveled all the way to London for. In the middle of the meeting, right out of the blue, it happened again, this infusion of golden light. I was operating in two worlds at once. Somehow I was able to bring the meeting to a positive conclusion, the Englishmen never suspecting I was being visited by the most sublime current of God's golden flow. That experience marked a turning point in my life, both materially (the deal I cut that day laid the foundation for my future successes) and spiritually. I knew from that point on I had to meditate. I'll show you where it all began, my life of meditation."

There was a door with a shiny brass handle in the corner behind the bathtub. He opened it and I followed him into a linen closet with thick wooden shelves of neatly ironed linens. "Here," he said, "this is where I began my inner work. It was in this closet, sitting on a cushion on the floor in the pitch dark, surrounded by the same sheets and towels that you see here today, that I began to meditate. I was a married man with three children. I owned factories. Yet the inner world fought to come out in me. Isn't that fantastic?"

Two of the mahayogi's sons had ganged up on the third, who was allied with their father. So when I was living in the house as the guest of the Mahayogi, I was also the guest of this son, Manoj, his wife Gita, and their seventeen-year-old son, Gautam. I'd see the other two brothers and their families and servants. I'd pass them in the vast hallways and staircases, but they would travel close to the opposite wall when we passed, never return my gaze, and wouldn't respond to my casual hellos. This was confusing at first since I still thought of it as the family's house. It was easier once I dealt with them as if they were strangers in a hotel.

Manoj had a home office, and I would go down there for long conversations which he'd conduct with one eye on the CNN business ticker tape running across the bottom of an outsized TV screen. Our conversations, which were frequently interrupted by calls to and from his stockbroker, usually started out on the topic of doing business in India. But no matter how they started, we'd always end up talking about his father, whom he referred to simply as Mahayogi.

"Mahayogi has always needed someone to serve him," Manoj said. "He used to travel by car. He had a driver then, and they would go across the country from north to south and they would stop at all the temples. Oh, you heard about his driver? Yes, he was a drunk. But what else could the poor fellow do? Mahayogi was in his visionary state the whole time, and the driver wasn't. The driver's only means of achieving an altered consciousness was alcohol. But in the end it didn't work out. He kept selling the car's parts and putting in cheaper ones. How else could he afford to keep himself drunk?

"Then there was this other fellow. He's younger than me. Now he calls himself Swami Brahmadev. He traveled with my father for something like eight years. My father made him what he is today.

"You know how my father is: he uses everyone as his servant. He used to have Swami Brahmadev, though he wasn't called Swami Brahmadev back then, running around for him, washing his clothes, making his food, preparing his tea. It would be two in the morning and Mahayogi would call out to him, 'Bring me tea,' and he would do it. Always. He was getting spiritual instruction from Mahayogi, but he was also Mahayogi's servant. That was fine at the beginning, but now it is causing problems. Mahayogi and I got the land for him to make an ashram for himself, and we constructed the place. And now the swami, that's what he calls himself, has a large following of people from all over the world—Russia, Columbia, Israel, France, Germany, Spain, the USA, Canada, Greece. And Swami Brahmadev is younger than I am! Whatever he is today, he must thank Mahayogi, my father.

"Now the problem is that sometimes Mahayogi suddenly appears at the ashram, and he still expects the swami to act as his servant. And the swami doesn't like it. I don't blame him. Even though we bought it for him and set it all up, the ashram is his. He's the big man there. But you know my father. He wouldn't hesitate to walk into the Prime Minister's office and order him to make tea. He's always expecting everyone to break the rules for him. The last time Mahayogi was there, the swami told him off. Now Mahayogi swears he'll never go back. He has nothing to do with the place. I still get letters from Swami Brahmadev. We talk on the phone. He's always trying to get me to come up to the ashram. With all these foreigners coming and looking up to him, I think he wants my business sense."

III

Circumstances brought me back to Bombay about one year later. This time, the mahayogi was not there; he was in his Himalayan stronghold. Since I had become friends with Manoj, his wife Gita, and son Gautam, I stayed at Krishna House as their guest. The mahayogi had given the bungalow's master bedroom, the huge wood-paneled room with finely carved and imposing teak furnishings and bay windows, to Gautam, which he and I shared during the course of my stay. Despite the considerable difference in our ages, we became fast friends, comfortable with each other as if we'd known each other for years. Gautam was a serious and brilliant student, and though the first fuzz of an incipient beard was just forming on his cheeks, he was intent on becoming an aerospace engineer. I think he saw this as his ticket out of Krishna House. His dream was to study in the United

States and work for NASA. Not for a moment did I think he wouldn't fulfill his dreams.

Gautam had just finished some important exams during which he studied so hard that he damaged his eyes, making them ultra-sensitive to light. In the vain attempt to determine whether his problem was physical or psychological (caused either by the intensity of his studying or the growing tensions within Krishna House), his mother was bringing him to one after another of the best eye doctors in Bombay. She had covered the room's huge bay windows with thick black paper as if she were expecting an air raid, plunging the room in perpetual twilight. And even though his exams were over, Gautam spent most of his time studying books of arcane mathematics and rocket propulsion. He sat at a desk in the farthest corner from the room's sole source of illumination, a low-wattage bulb protected by a linen shade with tassels. Wearing UV-protecting sunglasses, reading in a light that approximated that of deep space, it was easy to believe he was studying aerospace engineering in order to plot the course of his escape to a destination so far from Krishna House that it was beyond the pull of Earth's gravity.

Sometimes, when Gautam wasn't there, I'd peal back a corner of the black paper blocking the bay window to the front of the house just to let a few rays of light enter the room. I'd gaze out toward the Arabian Sea, a view obscured by what must be the world's largest birdhouse, which rose next door like a rotten tooth in the Bombay skyline. The neighborhood used to be comprised of bungalows like Krishna House. As far as I knew, Krishna House was the only bungalow in Breach Candy that hadn't been torn down to make way for a high-rise apartment building; this is because no other bungalow was mired in such internal fighting as to render its demolition impossible. Who said a house divided cannot stand? Next door must have been a house united, for the bungalow that once stood there had been razed. The high-rise that took its place was financed by those who would own the individual condominiums. When it was found to be three stories higher than city regulations permitted, they were ordered to demolish the top three floors. Since these top floors were already paid for by people awaiting the building's completion, they sued the builders. And since it takes at least a decade for a case to reach the Indian courts, construction on the building was simply stopped. This had all happened years before, leaving an empty concrete carcass reaching for the heavens and blocking the view of the Arabian Sea from Krishna House.

THE BIGGEST BIRDHOUSE IN THE WORLD

Nature abhors a vacuum.

Squatters, posing as security guards (or were they security guards who lived like squatters), took over the lower two floors, living the lives of slum-dwellers amid the fashionable millionaires at one of the best addresses in the city. I never knew whether they were merely tolerated or whether they were paid; either way they prevented human beings from inhabiting the upper floors, which were occupied by a variety of birds, mainly pigeons and swallows and crows, who went about their business catching insects, flying into the city in huge flocks in search of what could be gleaned from the city's streets, and raising their young—activities not entirely dissimilar to what you'd see in any high-rise: only the species was different. Above this huge birdhouse, vultures arched gracefully, awaiting an opportunity to dive for an easy meal.

Gautam was keenly aware of the hypocrisy of the adults around him, especially of his grandfather, the mahayogi.

GAUTAM

Though Gautam was removed by two generations from the mahayogi, Gautam lived very much in his shadow, as did everyone connected to him. Even though the mahayogi had been back in the Himalayas for over seven months at the time of my visit, his presence hung very much in the air of Krishna House. Every major aspect of Gautam's life had been determined by his being in the wake of the great man, though he never would have admitted it. The mahayogi had even named him. Gautam was the Buddha's given name.

"My grandfather," he said one day when we were lounging on the huge sofas in the perpetual twilight of the master bed-room, "he says he's a great yogi, but just look at him! What a nest of contradictions."

I found myself defending the mahayogi, even though I was thankful that he wasn't *my* grandfather, that the only role fate apportioned for me was that of being the scribe of his story and that his influence on me ended the moment I walked out the front door of Krishna House. From the first, I was struck by the mahayogi's greatness, even if it was alloyed with a certain madness. Maybe true greatness always has a hidden link to madness, like an unseen well. And it wasn't only his charisma, that divine favor some people seem to possess as if by a birth-right, drawing others to them. Never had I met anyone who could integrate such opposing natures in one human being. That the spiritual teacher of Jesus Christ could feel at home on the toilet reading the *Economic Times* I found astounding.

I told Gautam, "You should appreciate your grandfather. Only a great human being could integrate all that without bursting apart."

But Gautam would have none of it.

"I just want to get out of here," he said, clutching a book on jet propulsion, "as far away as I can."

IV

The last time I stayed at Krishna House the mahayogi was there. On my last evening, Manoj took the mahayogi,

Gita, Gautam, and me to the Breach Candy Club. The club, a few blocks away on the Arabian Sea, was *the* exclusive country club under the British. Since independence, it is still *the* country club in Bombay, exclusive to the point of having a board of trustees comprised of one token Indian and the rest foreigners. For a family to become members of the club, the one who applies has to hold a foreign passport. Gita was born in London. After years of wrangling, she and the family were finally allowed to join. I was allowed in as their guest.

The Breach Candy Club in the evening: the sun setting over the Arabian sea, the soft salt breeze churned by lazy fans, the sky's pink glow reflected in the huge swimming pool in the shape of India, liveried waiters delivering cocktails to parties sitting around tables overtopped with parasols set amid well-apportioned gardens, suntanned beauties stretched out on reclining lawn chairs clad in skimpy bikinis soaking in the sun's last rays, shipping magnates nonchalantly turning their heads at the passing of Bollywood stars. And then there was the entrance of the ocher-robed mahayogi.

To be a member of the party accompanying the mahayogi upon his entrance to the Breach Candy Club was how I would imagine it to be part of the entourage of George Harrison, the sitar-playing Beatle.

Heads turned at the entrance of Bollywood stars, but they were turned with a studied nonchalance, a forced casualness, as if to show that he whose head was turning was accustomed to the company of the stars. But a yogi in the Breach Candy Club—people lost all sense of decorum and stared. He couldn't be just *any* yogi. Had Deepak Chopra started wearing robes? Could it be the Maharishi himself? It was enough for him to enter a room for everyone to turn their heads. And this was true even before he took to the spiritual life. It was this quality, no doubt, that led to his meteoric rise from one of the hoards of the poverty stricken entering Bombay with dreams of riches to a jet-setting, cloth manufacturing magnate. Manoj described traveling with his father on his trips abroad when he was a boy. The mahayogi, dressed then in his hand-tailored suits, walking through the Vienna airport

with aplomb, would elicit stares and speculation. More than
once he was mistaken for Aristotle Onassis.

We were seated outside at a table lit by candles. The
sound of the surf was coming from the west and some soft
rock music coming from the east, from the direction of the
bar, which was becoming lively with the coming of night. A
waiter took our orders of gin and tonics, whiskey, and lem-
on water for the mahayogi. Gautam was allowed a beer. We
ate hot spicy fried potatoes for which the Breach Candy Club
was apparently famous.

A party of fashionable and sophisticated-looking Westerners sat down at the table next to ours. They ordered drinks
and food and started laughing and having a good time. You
could see them looking at the mahayogi and wondering just
who he might be, important enough to be having drinks out-
doors in the gentle breeze of the Arabian Sea at the Breech
Candy Club.

This did not escape the notice of the mahayogi. He pushed
back his chair at the head of our table and stood up with the
self-importance of the Chairman of the Board. Straightening
his robe, he strode confidently over to the table of fashionable foreigners. "Your table just looks *so* inviting," he said,
flashing that broad smile of his that never failed. The foreigners were of course delighted; just think, to have a yogi
sit at your table, right at the Breach Candy Club—and one
with such a beautiful smile and good teeth! In a flash, all the
men at the table stood up. The women flushed with delight.
They moved their chairs aside as one of the men got a chair
from another table. "Please," they sputtered as if in a single
voice, "we would be most delighted if you would join us." The
mahayogi puffed out his chest, considered it a moment, then
said with great aplomb, "Some other time—perhaps." And he
strode away.

Watching this, Manoj finished off his whiskey. "Where is he
going this time?" He asked no one in particular. When the mahayogi didn't return, Gita and Gautam went to find him. Gita
was especially worried he would create a scene and jeopardize
their membership at the Club, which they had spent years to

secure. "Foreign members can get away with murder here," she explained as she pushed back her chair. "But we Indians, we have to be careful." They had taken a calculated risk by bringing the mahayogi there. My departure made it a special occasion. They had risked it, and now he had gone missing.

Manoj snapped his fingers. A waiter came, and he ordered us another round of drinks. He was in a reflective mood. The topic, as always, was his father. "Mahayogi has always been a law unto himself," he said. "And he is always disappearing. When I was a boy he would leave for work in the morning. And then we'd get a call in the afternoon. He'd be at Sri Aurobindo's ashram in Pondicherry, on the other side of the subcontinent! Do you know Sri Aurobindo? He's dead now, but he was a great spiritual master. He started out as a freedom fighter, fighting British colonial rule. It was in a British jail that he started meditating. He wrote beautifully—he was the Shakespeare of the East.

"Why would anyone go to any other master? Even though he is dead, the spiritual technology is here. It is in the books by Sri Aurobindo. If you want to make plastics, shouldn't you go directly to DuPont? You can waste your time going to this company or that company, but it will not work out right. It's the same with spirituality: you can listen to this teacher or that teacher, but why bother when there was such a one as Aurobindo? Aurobindo offers the—what do you call it?—the superhighway to God. There are many little winding lanes. You can take one of them, but you'll end up lost."

While Manoj was talking, he was greeting people walking by, calling out to them by their first names. "I come here most days after work for a drink," he explained. "Often I eat dinner with my buddies as well." I knew this because Gautam had complained of the same, saying that his father didn't pay much attention to him or his mom. The disturbance in the household obviously penetrated his nuclear family as well.

"By the time my father was going to Sri Aurobindo's ashram," Manoj continued, "Aurobindo was already dead. But his spiritual collaborator was there; she was French, you know. They called her The Mother, The Pondicherry Mother. She, too, was extraordinarily wise, and very famous.

"So my father would set out to work one day and end up at the ashram in Pondicherry. Do you realize how extraordinary this is? Pondicherry is south of Madras, on the other side of India. He'd have left the house in his chauffeur-driven car on his way to one factory or another where his underlings would be gathered, awaiting an important meeting with the boss. And on the way, he'd suddenly get an inspiration and tell the driver to take him to the airport.

"Mahayogi was so rich that he never had even a single rupee in his pocket. That's how it is for rich people. They're not like us. They don't need money. They never have to buy a thing. They have servants for that. Money to a rich man is something dirty, something they wouldn't actually like to touch.

"So he'd have his driver drop him off at the Bombay airport. He'd bully himself into the office of the head of Indian Airlines, and convinced him to let him fly now and pay later. No one else on the planet could have gotten away with that. He must have negotiated in a similar fashion for the chauffeured car that brought him from the Madras airport to the ashram in Pondicherry, a drive of a few hours. I don't think anyone has ever successfully evaded my father's will.

"If you ever go to Pondicherry you will see how big the ashram is; it's an empire in itself. And everybody wanted to see The Mother. There were hundreds, thousands, every day. But when Mahayogi came, she'd immediately abandoned her schedule and give him a private audience. Sometimes, they would talk for hours. She was very impressed by him. Who wasn't?

"But anyway, one time when he arrived there and he had no money he went to the ashram cashier and told him he wanted to present some money to The Mother and therefore he told the cashier to give him 10,000 rupees. He promised to have the money wired as soon as he returned to Bombay. This was highly irregular, but you know how it is: you can't say no to Mahayogi! It's simply impossible. So the cashier gave my father 10,000 rupees, which was a lot of money in those days. A fortune. Mahayogi gave the money to The Mother. The next day Mahayogi went to the cashier again. 'I am about to see The Mother and I want to present her with another 10,000 rupees. Please give it to me and I promise to have the money sent upon my arrival in Bombay.' The cashier gave it to him; but since The Mother had given the 10,000 rupees he had presented to her the day before back to the cashier, Mahayogi gave the same 10,000 rupees to The Mother. On the third day Mahayogi asked the cashier again for 10,000 rupees. 'How am I going to enter this in the books?' the cashier despaired; but what could he do? It was Mahayogi. For the third time Mahayogi gave the same 10,000 rupees to The Mother."

Manoj drained half his glass in a single gulp.

"Yes, my father has had the most extraordinary luck in everything he has done, as if he has been called upon by the gods for greatness. One can only speculate why the gods choose one man and not another. I have no such luck. If anything, I have been cursed by coming in the wake of Mahayogi. It is true that when Mahayogi was a boy he had a guru, a great guru, who could see the past, present, and future. The guru told him that whatever he touched would turn to gold. And he was right. Everything he did made money. My father's timing has always been impeccable.

"For instance, when he abandoned his business affairs for the Himalayas, he slipped away just as the noose was tightening. Everything was mired in the courts, and suddenly it was all in the hands of me, my brothers, and my father's business partner. He took on this partner early on. Maybe you've seen him, lurking in the hallways. He also lives at Krishna House—he's the older guy that lives with his wife just down the hall from Mahayogi's room. He too has been lucky. He didn't have such a touch as my father. He's just been along for the ride. Mahayogi needed someone to do his leg work and he picked this man. It was this man's good karma that connected him with my father. From the beginning it has all been Mahayogi's doing."

Manoj ordered a third drink.

"Early on, when my father and his partner were just getting under way, they had a load of Egyptian cotton coming in on a ship. Somehow the ship sank, right here, off Bombay. They had everything invested in that shipment, and without it they would be ruined. It was insured, but business being what it is in India, they had vastly undervalued the shipment for customs purposes, and the insurance would not cover a fraction of its value.

"Things are not that different now. We own quite a bit of property, and we rent some of it out. But in India, you have to lie; you have to cheat, just to survive. If you rent out property you have to pay so much tax that you lose money. If you tell the tax man the truth, you lose. So you have to cook the books—you have to lie. You have to cheat.

"Anyway, I was talking about Mahayogi and his business partner and how their shipment of cotton was lost at the bottom of Bombay's harbor. What to do? They went to Mahayogi's family guru for help, and asked him to pray for them. The guru said all he could do was pray to the goddess. It would be up to her. He told the partner to hold out his hand. He placed on the partner's hand a sweet, one of those round sweet balls made of milk and sugar. Then he had the partner close his fingers around it and hold it over the guru's head while the guru repeated the goddess's holy mantra. He said if by the end of the prayer the ball was gone, all would turn out well. But if the ball was still there, there would be nothing to be done. So the partner held the ball in his closed fist over the guru's head while the guru said his mantras to the goddess. When he was finished, the partner opened his hand and the ball was gone! Somehow it had disappeared.

"With time, the boat was lifted from the water. The cotton was in huge bales held with iron rings. To recoup their loss, they had to go through the expense of opening the bales and drying the cotton. But the cotton was no longer white. It had turned a light shade of yellow from being at the bottom of the sea and from the iron rings. They had rusted, you see.

"But even this turned out in his favor: when they went to sell the cotton, the cloth manufactures loved it! The cotton was exactly the color that was all the rage at that time, just off white, slightly yellow. Look at Bollywood films of the 40's and you'll see they wore clothes of that particular color. And Mahayogi used to wear that color shirt too. People would turn and look, 'Who is that man?' He always dressed in the finest suits. So they sold that cotton, and they made a tremendous profit. Because, you see, the cloth manufacturers didn't have to dye the cotton. The sea had done that. The only problem was that when they went to sell their next shipment, the manufacturers all wanted the same yellowed cotton. They could neither give them more nor explain how they achieved the first shipment.

"Yes, everything Mahayogi touched turned to gold. And though his guru said it would, he never said Mahayogi wouldn't mismanage it. He only said he would acquire the gold. The mismanagement of the funds was entirely Mahayogi's own work. No one said it wouldn't pass through his fingers.

"When Mahayogi suddenly left for the Himalayas, he left everything in a mess, and my brothers, they wanted to retire. They expected the checks to just keep rolling in without lifting a finger. I saw early on that someone would have to act quickly not to lose everything. So I jumped into the fray and took on the responsibility. If I hadn't, we would have all ended up in ruin. I've had to curb their lifestyles. And for this I earned the respect of my father (that's why we're still close) and the hatred of my brothers. There have been plots for murder in our house. Just the other day one of my brothers attacked Mahayogi. He caught himself at the last moment and fled from the room. They've even resorted to black magic against Gita and me. We had to have a Hindu priest come and exorcise the evil they planted. The spells they cast were so powerful that it took the priest many days and cost us tens of thousands of rupees.

"The only way not to lose everything was to sell off some factories in order to consolidate and invest the money, but we couldn't. We couldn't agree, and besides, everything was mired in legal battles and court cases. My father couldn't have gone for his spiritual retreat at a worse time. I'm still the only one of my brothers who works. The others just accept the checks as if it were their birthright.

"I sometimes wonder what it's all about, what's the purpose of all this that we've gone through, why Mahayogi was singled out by fate, and why I have to spend my life stitching things together and avoiding murder plots hatched by my brothers. I see what Mahayogi's done and I see he's on the right course, to try to reunite with god. But now I'm too busy, too bound up in worldly things—responsibilities, investments, the factories. I suppose it is true, what the wise ones say, that to reach God you have to surrender. Surrender everything. Unless you give everything up and go out with only your begging bowl, you will not make it. No way someone like me could make it, not here in Bombay."

Manoj lifted his whiskey, drained it, and ordered a fourth. He watched a bird gliding in the onshore wind. "Sometimes I try to understand what it's all about," he said, "why we all have to go through this. I think about it every day. And I know it's not even for him. I know that in the end I'll have to build the Krishna temple."

"Krishna temple," I asked, "what Krishna temple?"

"Mahayogi is a great devotee of Krishna. He named his factory Krishna's Mill; the house is called Krishna House. When he left for the Himalayas, he said that he wanted his share—when it clears the courts—to be used to build a Krishna temple. He spent his entire life amassing a fortune, and in the end the fortune is for Krishna. I'm convinced this is all Krishna's doing. It's the only way I can make sense out of any of it. All else is incidental—living in a house full of plots and intrigues, this wrangling through the courts; in the end the only worthwhile outcome of the entire affair, the only thing of any lasting value, will be the Krishna temple."

Just then Gita and Gautam returned.

"Where's Mahayogi," Manoj asked, wearily.

"We looked everywhere," Gita said. "Finally we found him sitting by himself on the grass on the other side of the pool and facing the sea. He was meditating. We didn't dare disturb him."

THE AUTHOR WITH THE MAHAYOGI
AT THE GANDHI ASHRAM, KAUSANI 1999

DEFENDER OF THE DHARMA
TALES OF A BUDDHIST MURDERER

MONSOON IN DARJEELING

It was a late mid-February afternoon in Darjeeling. The Himalayan town, at almost 8,000 feet, had been in the clouds for weeks. It had become my habit as the sky began to darken towards evening to quit my desk and wander the damp, cold, and foggy back alleyways of the market with my camera. I would go back beyond the vegetable dealers, to the wooden stalls selling everything from tea and tools to spices to books. In odd corners, back where the tailors with their treadle sowing machines punctuated the sloshing sound of running water with their rat-a-tat-tat, I would render myself inconspicuous, which wasn't difficult since everything dissolved into the gloom. And there I would capture a succession of cloaked figures and women wrapped in damp shawls appear out of the gray fog only to dissolve back into it.

It was down in the market on just such a late afternoon that I first saw him. I was looking through my camera's viewfinder, and I thought my eyes were playing tricks on me. Only the hardiest of travelers make it as far as Darjeeling in winter, people with a reason for being there. I was spending the winter in Darjeeling for a book I was writing, though I was taking a break from writing to photograph in the alley, trying to render myself invisible with my camera, making the best of bad weather by photographing the interplay of figure and fog. I hadn't seen a tourist in weeks.

From the first I knew he was American. What struck me was how average he looked, like a typical middle-aged American guy, rounded, balding, what hair he did have was crew cut. He wore a light-gray windbreaker with a corporate logo and loafers. His loafers were soggy and encrusted in mud. He looked cold and out of place. His face wore an expression of surprise, as if his Chevy had broken down somewhere outside Kansas City and he suddenly found himself walking down an alleyway in the middle of a cloud. The majority of Americans never leave North America. Two thirds don't even have a passport. This man looked like part of that majority.

So startled was I to see him in my camera's viewfinder that I took the camera from my eye, just to see if he existed outside the world within my viewfinder. He did, and he came right up to me.

"If you think this is bad," he said, sounding a little like a stand-up comedian, "it's even worse in Gloom—I mean Ghoom." Ghoom, a town a few miles from Darjeeling, was the wettest place I knew. A cloud hung there even when the sun shone everywhere else. The sun hadn't shown itself in Darjeeling in weeks. Ghoom must have been miserable.

"My lama is down there, staying at the monastery," he continued. "God, it was horrible. The fog was so thick I got lost, right in the courtyard. I'm still chilled to the bone. You know what pilots say who fly in the Himalayas: You have to be careful, the clouds have rocks in them." He laughed heartily at his own joke. He did not fit my idea of someone with a lama in Ghoom.

He put out his hand with the assertiveness of a traveling salesman. "The name is Stephen McCain," he said. I introduced myself. He admired my camera, which was an old classic, and told me he worked in the film industry.

"Do you know where one can get shelter from this weather," he asked, "and maybe something to eat?"

I knew of a place close by, the Shangri-La Restaurant, upon whose back wall was painted a huge mural of da Vinci's Last Supper, with Buddha sitting in for Christ and monks in burgundy robes with shaved heads taking the place of the twelve disciples. It was getting too dark to photograph anyway, so I led the way to the Shangri-La. As my reward, he offered to buy me something to drink.

Since we were the only customers, we chose the table next to the fireplace, which the waiter filled with chunks of coal and lit for us. We ordered rum and hot water. As the fire took, steam rose from our clothes.

THE LAST SUPPER, PAINTED BY MAHENDRA THAMI

He asked a bit about me, and what I was doing in Darjeeling, but I could tell he was distracted. His right leg was jittering and his eyes were darting furtively around the room. I had the sense he was less interested in hearing my story than in telling his own.

"I've done many things in this life," he said. "Now I'm on the lama circuit with Geshela—that's my lama. He lives in the States, you see, and I'm his lead disciple. I've been with him the longest, more than fifteen years. We asked him how long he'll live. He doesn't think that long, maybe another five years. He's in his eighties, you see. That's why we're here: to take him to his old haunts, the monasteries where he lived, so he can see his old friends one last time. I've done enough in this lifetime to fill a few incarnations. Now I'm a filmmaker, but I've done many things. I even used to work for the PLO."

His rapid fire of words ended suddenly with the staccato of those three letters representing the Palestinian Liberation Organization. Maybe he had said too much. I asked him what he did for the PLO.

He took a sip of his drink, glanced around the room to make sure no one was within earshot, and leaned forward.

"It's a long story," he said in a hushed tone, "but I started by smuggling hashish from Morocco and Tunisia. This must have been in '68. I was driving a van in Tunisia and the police caught me and brought me to the police station. And there I was in cuffs next to my van, my hashish piled up on the sidewalk, about a hundred bystanders looking on. I thought, O-oh, I'm in trouble this time. There was a lot of money in that shipment—and the money wasn't mine. I could bribe my way out of jail, but I needed the hash too. So I had to do some fancy negotiation. I insisted on speaking with the big boss, the district commissioner of police. They brought me to him, but my problem was to find a solution mutually beneficial *and* acceptable to us both. You see, you have to find a way to make the other guy save face. You can't just come out and bribe such an official, not someone that high. He has his dignity.

"Then I hit upon an idea.

"So I say to him, 'Do you have a son?'

"He says, 'Yes.'

"I say, 'Has he made his haj?' You know, the haj, that's the pilgrimage to Mecca. He says, no his son hasn't made his haj. So I say, 'Don't you think I could make a contribution towards your son's haj?' The commissioner smiled a crooked smile, as if my hook got him right in the lip! So I ask him how much a ticket would cost to Mecca and he tells me and I say, 'No, a first class ticket.' I was out of there in no time. And for the next couple of years, I sent many a police official's son on his haj.

"The finest hash wasn't from North Africa, though; it was from Lebanon. So I started smuggling hash from Lebanon. In Lebanon it was mostly the Palestinians selling the hash. Their struggle, just to survive, took money, and more traditional methods of making money were closed to them. Remember, I had spent a long time in Muslim countries and had many Muslim friends. I must have gained lots of good Muslim karma by sending so many fine and outstanding sons of high North African police officials on their haj.

"Smuggling arms or drugs—it wasn't that different. Many of the same skills. I was in my twenties—I'm in my mid fifties now—and I was idealistic, fighting the good fight. Or so I thought. When you're young, you have lots of energy. I was smuggling shipments of high-powered weapons. Once I even delivered a shipment for the Black Panthers. We stole them from an armory in North Carolina and drove them to the West Coast.

"The whole world was on fire. Vietnam was raging. People were freaking out all over the place. It couldn't go on forever. For me the end came when I got busted with a shipment of guns for the PLO. The PLO were both honorable and loyal. They busted me out of jail and helped me flee the country."

Stephen laughed nervously. "That was all very long ago." It seemed he had said more than he meant to.

Hardly missing a beat, he changed the subject.

"I believe we all have many incarnations in this very life. In this one, I'm with Geshela. He's been in the States a long time, you see. He's on the lama circuit there—you know retreats, the whole thing. Our retreats are by donation only.

By relying on peoples' consciences, you get more. Most put in $100. We have a hundred people. That's $10,000. For a weekend. Not bad wages."

Stephen McCain cracked a wry smile.

"To tell you the truth," he said after a while, "though he wears a simple monk's robe, Geshela's a rich little fellow."

"How do you think the money and the West affect him?" I asked him

"I think he plays into it. They all do.

"These Tibetans are a bit like children," he said, laughing. "Right there in the moment. They're probably the most developed human beings the earth has ever produced; but socially— and especially sexually—they're unsophisticated. They're really mountain people, you know. And then they go to the West and the women fawn over them. They can have their pick."

Stephen shifted constantly on his chair and ran his hand over his closely cropped, bristly hair. He wiped beads of perspiration off his forehead and upper lip as he told his tales at breakneck speed.

I asked him how he dealt with the elaborate ritual, all the demons and gods, in Tibetan Buddhism.

"That's a problem, even for me," he said. "Actually I'm a Theravadan—you know, that's the southern branch of Buddhism. I first encountered Buddhism in Cambodia, where it's all much cleaner and to the bone. No gods, nothing. Just meditation and cleaning the mind. Later, I lived in Sri Lanka, with my second wife. My daughter was conceived there. I've been married three times, you see. Long story. Have two children. A son who's twenty-nine. My daughter's now nineteen. And Geshela kids me. I've been with him fifteen years now and he says, 'Stephen, you're still a Theravadan.' So I say, 'When will you convert me?'

"So I ask Geshela: You can pick your parents for your next life, right? And he says yes, if he wants. He's known my daughter since she was four. I named her Alexandria because of Lawrence Durrell's Quartet. Did you know that Lawrence Durrell went to school here, in Darjeeling? That's right; he went to Saint Joseph's, just up the road.

"Anyway, the first time I brought my daughter to meet Geshela she asked me if he was going to be like a raisin, all bald and wrinkled. I told her, yes.

"So I bring her to him—this was in the States—and there were many people there and I had to speak to someone. I lost track of her and then there she was with Geshela in the next room sitting on the floor playing jacks. Ever since, they've had a special closeness.

"So I say to him, 'If you can pick your next mother after you die, why don't you wait a few years and then pick Alexandria? She'll be of child-bearing age, and she'd be a good mother for you.' His face lit up with the thought. He really beamed with the idea. 'Yes,' he said, 'I think I'll do that!'

"But then I told him, 'If she's your mother, then I'll be your grandfather—and it'll be payback time!' His face turned red; from his chin, it moved up right to the top of his shaved head. 'Oh—no,' he said, 'oh, no!'"

Stephen McCain laughed a staccato laugh, wiped the sweat from his lip, and changed the subject:

"Everything has its purpose, you know. Even our meeting. It's not often we meet someone on this level. There's a reason our paths have crossed. Can't you feel it? There *are* no coincidences."

Though strange to say it, I knew what he meant. He was some sort of madman with a motor mouth, intent on telling the mad tale of his life by stitching the disparate facts of the universe together into a unified whole, making connections like flashes of lightning, hugely powerful, yet ephemeral.

Out the window a bevy of Western women passed by in the darkening gloom, shaved headed, in the robes of Tibetan nuns. When I turned back to Stephen McCain, he had a strange look on his face.

"I know what it's like to kill a man," he said. "I know the feeling of a knife going into flesh. The first time it was difficult. It weighed on me. But then, well, you have to defend yourself...

"The whole problem of humanity is courage. Fear—that's the block. I've always defended myself. The only difference now is that I've taken the bodhisattva vow, the Buddhist vow of love and compassion for all sentient beings. I'm a follower of the Tibetan dharma—the sacred teachings, the Way.

"I have defended my life—with death. Now I am a defender of the dharma."

I asked him what the circumstances were when he killed a man.

For the first time, Stephen McCain fell silent. He closed his eyes and rocked gently in his seat, rather like an inmate in an asylum. A full minute went by. Then, with eyes still closed, he started nodding his head. He opened his eyes.

"I've rarely spoken of this. My three wives know, two or three close friends. My children don't even know. I haven't spoken of it in years.

"It was after I got into trouble in the States, with the guns and all, and been busted out by the PLO. They got me out of the country—and there was no way I could return. Nor did I want to.

"America.

"America was waging war in Southeast Asia, shredding villages in Vietnam. It was also the time of the secret bombing of Cambodia. And *they* considered *me* a fugitive from justice? I had grown up the son of a career military man: World War II vet, American Legion—the whole thing. I saw how the war had destroyed him. And now America was doing it again, sacrificing their young on the altar of war.

"The war had done a job on my father, psychologically, and in turn he did a job on me and my three brothers. My youngest brother was a heroin addict. When he was nineteen he said to me, 'I'm not going to stick around here for long.' I asked him what he meant. 'I'm opting out. There's too much pain down here.' Two months later, he was dead of an overdose.

"Yeah, I've seen a lot of death—and more than my share of destruction. My godfather and godmother both committed suicide."

The pained look that crossed his face lifted almost instantly, leaving a philosophic glow.

"It's all karmic, the life one leads. Even one's death, one's pain. I told you, I'm a defender. It's true that I've killed to defend myself. Buddhism has turned me into a defender of the dharma—though I could kill again, if I needed to. The stance of the true warrior is always one of defense, never offense. All true warriors know this. And I was bred for it. I'm a Scott; I come from four generations of military men.

"After I married my German wife, I told my brothers we had to forgive Dad. You see, his problem was that as a soldier he had killed a lot of innocent people. This embittered him and made him an alcoholic, and we all hated him. But you know, you get older—and maybe a bit wiser?—and by then I had been with Buddhism a long time, so I thought we should have compassion for him and forgive. Dad was old by then, and all alone. My brothers refused. So I went myself to see him—where else but at the American Legion Hall. He was drinking with his buddies and they all knew I was married to a German, and none of them would look me in the eye. All they would do is stare into their glasses of Budweizer. But not because of why you'd think, because I had married the 'enemy.' They were ashamed in front of me. They knew they had killed innocent people. Just think of Dresden and the firebombs. This is what bonded them, what kept them knocking back the beers. Not the glory. If it were only the glory, they could have gotten on with their lives. No, it was the horror of war, the death they had delivered to innocent people, to women and children.

"And that the kid of a buddy of theirs was married to a German woman brought it all back, the memories beer could not erase. All they could do was drink more beer and wish for stronger medicine."

Stephen lifted his glass, but before it could reach his lips the next idea flashed through his mind, demanding expression.

"And compared to the soldiers of Vietnam, they were mature when they went to war. Did you know the average age of a soldier in World War II was twenty-six? In Vietnam, it was nineteen. But they had stronger medicine. They had heroin and ganja.

"After I got caught with the guns and was busted out of jail by the PLO, the PLO helped me out of the country. I had had some pretty rough characters after me before, but now I was a wanted man, a big enough fish that I was on the FBI's short list. The CIA were expending resources on me as well.

"I was in my mid-twenties. I didn't care whether I lived or died. Actually, I thought I was invincible, that nothing and no one could touch me. I had been in sticky situations. And, yes, I had even killed. Yet I was always the one to survive. Now I was in flight from the United States government, and where better to flee than to the center of the maelstrom, to the very heart of dark violence.

"So I went to Cambodia.

"The country my country was bombing was going to teach me about peace. It was in Cambodia that I first encountered Buddhism."

Stephen sipped his drink and looked into the fire. Then he caught my eye.

"I was traveling through the countryside, the hot, steamy Cambodian jungle, when the Americans started carpet bombing. I was staying in villages, always on the move, sleeping in Buddhist monasteries, trying to stay one step ahead of America's bombing raids. This was 1969-70. The stench of death was everywhere.

"I found a peaceful place, a village in the jungle. I stayed there about a month, got to know the people. And then we saw the formations of bombers; we heard the distant rumblings, then the bombs exploding in the neighboring villages. We were next. There was a bus in the village, and a bunch of us jumped in. We had gone a few miles when we heard above the engine's roar the sound of the missiles coming in—a high whine followed by silence, which ended in tremendous explosions whose impact blew out the bus's windows. The sides of the road exploded. Everybody panicked. The driver froze. He didn't know what to do. Bombs were exploding now one after the other in long lines.

"If I had learned anything in my life till that point it was how to act in a situation of life and death. So I ran to the front of the bus, peeled the drivers' fingers from the wheel, grabbed him by the shoulders, and threw him out of his seat.

"I was now responsible for a busload of souls that the entire might of the US Air Force was hell-bent on killing.

"Since the bombs were pressing forward before us, I thought the safest place was back in the village. So I turned the bus around. And when we got to the village, the village was in ruins. There were craters everywhere, half the size of this restaurant.

"We staggered out of the bus, and the trees were filled with shredded meat. It was impossible to tell which meat was human and which of it was water buffalo."

Stephen closed his eyes and tears ran down his cheeks. "I'm sorry, man" he said. "I've only spoken of this a few times."

He collected himself and continued: "Then we heard the unmistakable sound of choppers coming in—you know the sound."

His face lit up. He was suddenly the stand-up comedian. "You know the mantra of Cambodia in those times, don't you? 'Chicka.' The sound of helicopter rotors. Chicka—chicka—chicka—chicka."

He howled with a sudden burst of laughter like machine gun fire. The tears running down his cheeks were for this brief moment tears of laughter. He wiped them with the back of his hands and continued.

"Two helicopters came in over the village and landed. We were all too stunned and in shock to do anything—neither to fear nor to hide. And out of the helicopters came these American Southern Baptist fundamentalist missionary medics. They were there because they were Christians and felt it their duty to administer to the wounded.

"Remember, this was Nixon's dirty little secret, his bombing of Cambodia. And mind you, they had come in with about $300,000 worth of equipment, all from passing the hat in churches in Alabama and Mississippi and who knows where else.

"I went with one of the nurses—she had the sweetest Mississippi accent—and assisted her with the wounded. The whole time I thought they'd take me with them. I thought I was saved, being a white guy like them and an American. But when they started up the rotors and I began running with the nurse toward the chopper, she grabbed my arm and stopped.

"She looked me right in the eye. 'We can't take you,' she said.

"I was stunned. Smoke from a distant town rose on the horizon. She pointed to it and said they were headed there to do their good works. 'It is all we can do to lift ourselves and our supplies,' she said. 'We can't even take the wounded. We can't afford the weight.'

"For the first time in a long while I cared whether I lived or died.

"The nurse said, 'Over there, in that direction, is Thailand. It should be a three-day's walk. Stay off the trails and travel only at night, and by the grace of Jesus the Lord, you'll make it.' And I did. I walked to Thailand."

Stephen drained his glass.

"What happened that day in the Cambodian jungle changed me forever. There was America, in the guise of B-52s, bombing the shit out of the country, shredding innocent Buddhist villagers and leaving their meat hanging in trees—all to protect civilization from the godless commies; and there was America, in the guise of fundamentalist Christians, coming in to mop up after them, performing their Christian duty in hundreds of thousands of dollars worth of equipment gathered by church donations, no doubt from good commie-hating, flag-waving bible thumpers. You never heard of this in the press, did you? But I was there.

"It renewed my faith in America. It was in the jungles of Cambodia suffering America's secret bombing that I experienced the greatness of America's diversity. That both extremes could exist at one time changed me forever—maybe because I was myself a nest of such contradictions. But I'll tell you a secret—we all are.

"And by the very fact that America is still wreaking havoc with the world at the same time that we are sitting here, in a cloud in the Himalayas, connecting at such a high level—this speaks to the fact that the planet is changing fast. It's all coming to fruit. There must be thousands of other conversations just like this taking place all over the world—at this very moment! We're not the only ones pushing the envelope; it takes many minds, in joint effort, to think new thoughts.

"Look: the Tibetans have the dharma, perhaps the greatest kernel of ancient wisdom to survive to the modern age; but in the past they hoarded it, they kept it for themselves. They also had a rigid social system—vast landholders (often the high incarnate lamas) and their tenant-slaves. They had internal wars going on all the time, often between monasteries! They fought so much amongst themselves that when the Chinese invaded, they couldn't unite against them.

"It is because the Tibetans fled Tibet and have been scattered around the planet that the dharma has spread. Without the Chinese slaughter, my lama wouldn't have left Tibet. Without him, I wouldn't have gotten the teachings. I wouldn't be here. I probably would have killed myself long ago. The Tibetans protected this ancient kernel of wisdom for millennia. Now they're sharing it with the world. The Chinese gave them the push. These teachings could just save the planet yet. And for that, we'd have to thank the Chinese.

"Don't get me wrong," he said, "I don't condone what the Chinese did in Tibet. But I don't like all this complaining about it either, especially among Western Buddhists, who idealize everything Tibetan. Look, two out of six million Tibetans were murdered by the Chinese. Do you really think the Tibetans had nothing to do with it? When it's one's karma to kill, it's another's karma to die. What's the law of karma worth if it only holds for when good happens? When something bad happens and you don't see how you've brought it on, it's only because you don't see the connections. That's the law of karma: everything's connected. Everything!"

Stephen McCain's Midwestern salesman's exterior seemed but a disguise, for there was something all-encompassing about his vision, the way he explained how both butchers and saints are needed for humanity's new dawn, how if only one hundredth of one percent of humanity understood the tenets of wisdom and compassion as handed down by the Tibetans, that's all it would take. One hundredth of one percent—critical mass to turn the whole thing around. He believed nothing could stop it now. He saw a new dawn. And in his presence, I saw it too.

"Look, I'm a film maker," he said. "See it from third camera, from that objective place, like God looking down. The lamas travel now to every country on earth, teaching love and compassion. Think of how small their number is next to the total six billion.

"It's all a big play," he said. "We're all just out here on the planet—but we're only here on parole!"

Stephen McCain reached across the table and put his hand on my shoulder. He squeezed so hard I had to keep myself from wincing. I couldn't help but thinking that the greatness of a man may be known by the breadth of his contradictions.

When we got up to leave, Stephen McCain told me he was going to Nepal early the next morning with Geshela. We shook hands outside the restaurant. Then we hugged each other. We stood with our palms pressed in an attitude of prayer, knowing it was unlikely we'd ever meet again.

It was then I realized he had never told me the circumstances under which he had killed. I was going to say something when I saw what was written on his windbreaker, what I had taken for a corporate logo. It was from a film he had worked on. In big letters it said, THE GUILTY ONE. And under, in smaller letters, was written, CREW.

The Interior of a Dot

Not long ago I was in Dharamsala, the Indian hill station that serves as the Himalayan exile home of the Dalai Lama. My camera was slung under my open jacket, and I was practicing my particular method of photography, which entails my becoming invisible. While I don't believe in literal invisibility—at least I haven't achieved such yet—I have on occasion come close. I've stood in the middle of a busy Indian market and taken a portrait of someone at close range when something approaching magic occurs. Though the person passing in front of my lens was fully aware that he was being photographed at the moment the shutter clicked, and had even given his tacit approval, there was something in it, almost a magic, such that if someone were to have asked him a moment later if I'd taken his photo I'm certain he would have retained no conscious memory of it, the moment it had occurred in having passed without a trace.

When out on my photographic excursions I move slowly in a state of deep concentration, my shutter ready, my eyes ever vigilant, slowing time in order to capture that 250th of a second slice. It is a form of meditation in which the visual predominates over the other senses to an extraordinary degree; the ideal is to be awareness itself: eyes wide open. Occasionally I've come close.

The most interesting part of the market in which to photograph was a place where five roads come together in a great mix of people and cars, taxis, trucks, and busses. Pack horses also pass through this intersection, as do cows, dogs, donkeys, and humans of every description. Monks brush shoulders with Israeli Rastafarians. Sometimes there are even monkeys swinging from the wires overhead, making their way across the landscape.

Western Buddhist practitioners, Taiwanese sponsors, backpacking travelers, Indian tourists, monks, nuns, lamas, porters, businessmen, beggars, merchants, and—if the truth be known—the occasional Chinese spy, all have good reason to pass through this busy crossroads in the course of their day.

I had been there a while this particular afternoon when I noticed looking at me, from under a black felt hat and beneath bushy eyebrows, a long-haired Indian gentleman of questionable repute. He was clutching an artist's satchel. I had half noticed him

hovering in the background as I photographed, standing at a slight distance as if distracted by the busy passage of people, yet always close enough to give the impression he was observing me, as if trying to intuit my photographic method. He appeared like this a few too many times for it to be

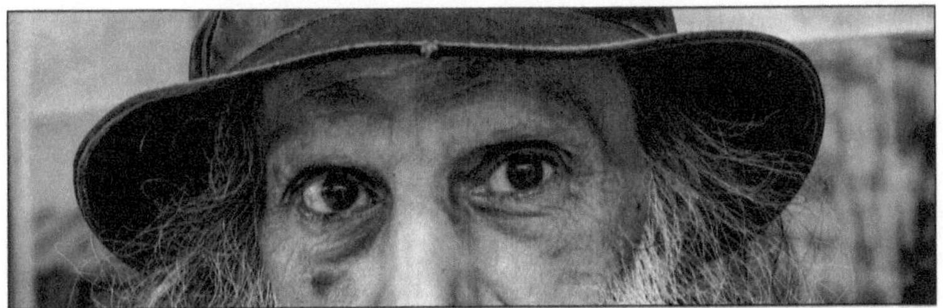

chance. There was something nervous about him, as if he lacked something he hoped to find on the street. I did not feel like mingling with him, and as many times as he drew close, I moved away.

He picked his moment to approach me. Without my being aware, he stood exactly out of my field of vision, behind my shoulder blades like a thief.

"How do you do," he said. His accent was Indian, yet had something in it of the British upper crust.

I pretended not to hear. He then said something about memory, or that he remembered me, but since I didn't turn I couldn't be certain it was me he was addressing, or at least I could deny it, so I stepped away feigning interest in a sweet shop on the corner. He had held back so subtly that my eyes

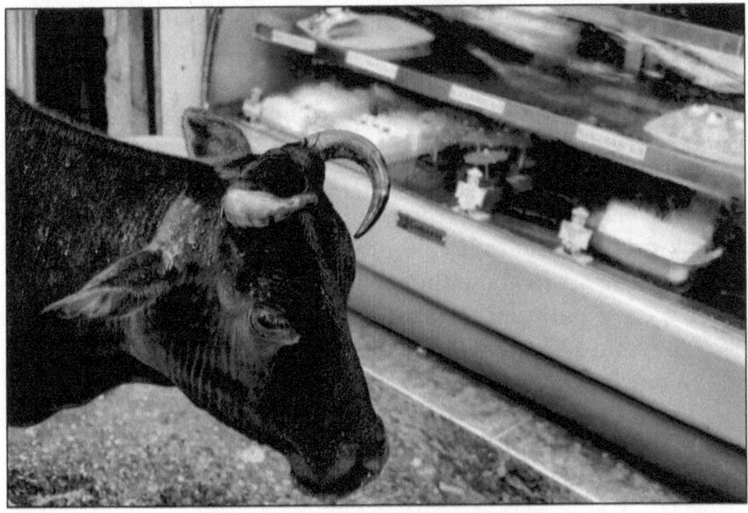

A Cow Eyeing a Sweet Shop

had never quite settled on him. Since I didn't now want to turn and look, he remained a moving shadow.

Some time later this long-haired gentleman came up to me again. This time he appeared at a more friendly angle and was standing just beside me when I turned. This time I could hear what he was saying.

"If I should remember you," he said, "*how* should I remember you?"

"*Why* should you remember me?" I asked, suspicious of what he wanted.

"*Why* is not the question. That is a seven-year-old boy's question. They're always asking, 'Why, why, why...' I've seen you, and now we've spoken—so certainly will I remember you. Therefore, the question is not *why*. I ask how. *How* should I remember you? As a photographer?—I've seen you with your camera; as a lover of humanity?—I've seen your eye. Or perhaps you are a musician?"

"I am not a musician," I said.

"May I invite you to a cup of tea?"

"I just had one."

"I am asking you to a cup of tea," he said, becoming a little testy, "because I'd like to open a conversation."

I didn't fancy going with this stranger. With the sun not far from setting, the light was becoming interesting.

"How should *I* remember *you*?" I asked.

"My friend," he said, his voice edged again with irritation, "that is why I want to invite you to tea."

I said nothing. He continued: "I have my store of paintings in here," he said, indicating the black case he was clutching. "I've brought them today because it is my friend's 60th birthday and I want to show them to him.

"You're a painter?" I asked.

"Yes, and I also write."

"What do you write?"

"For four years now I've been writing a book; four years— or has it been eight?"

He laughed at the irony of his imprecise notion of time.

"The theme of the work is the spiritual in art. It was a

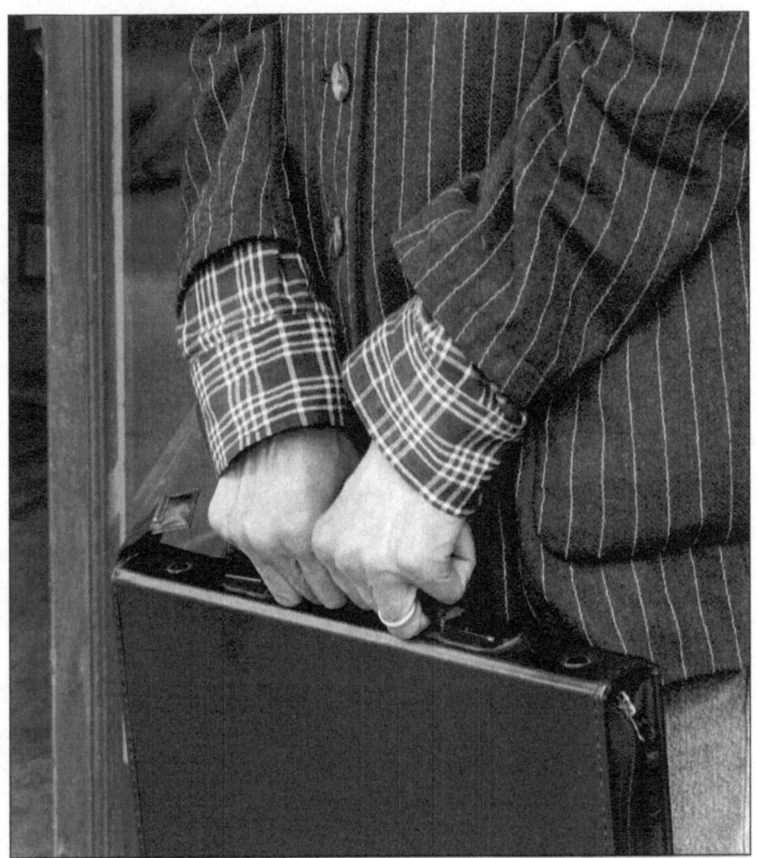

question posed by the abstract impressionist painter Wassily Kandinsky. For this work I've had to read a lot—especially 19th and 20th century philosophers from the West, which I believe is your side of the world. I also know Sanskrit quite well and read in Eastern Philosophy—Hinduism, Vedanta, and the rest. The philosophers of the East can sometimes make your Western philosophers look like children, you know.

"I also play the drum, and I sing English poetry. All the metaphysical poets. Almost everybody: Wordsworth, Shakespeare, William Blake.

"It is because of my book that I have come here to

Dharamsala—to have the silence of the mountains in which to write. Only when it is done, only then can I go to the market with my paintings."

"You want to sell your paintings?"

"I want to bring them to the public's attention—and to get my pound of gold, and my glory. But fame and fortune can never be our true aim. That is why our psychology calls them *extrinsic* motivations. If the artist is an artist—and this applies to the spiritual man as well—the motivation for his work must solely be *intrinsic*, coming from within."

He snapped open his case and took out his portfolio of tiny paintings in the plastic leaves of a loose leaf binder.

"I used to work with watercolors," he said, "as well as oils, colored pencils, and even charcoal. But for a long time now I've worked only with a ballpoint pen, such as you buy for five rupees in the market."

He showed me the first painting, which was tiny, smaller than a playing card.

"A friend of mine, from when I was living in Paris, looked at my paintings one day and reminded me that I was Indian. He was saying I had been unduly influenced by my time in the West, and that it showed in my paintings. He challenged me to paint my traditional motifs. So I took up the challenge and put the holy cow in a wholly new perspective. Look, I will show you.

Carefully, he pulled the painting from the plastic sheath and held it in the palm of his hand.

"This took me six weeks to complete," he said, "up to eight hours a day. It shows the irony of pop art. Can you see? It's a cow showing her ass."

It took a moment to make it out, but there is was, a nicely executed cow's ass presenting itself to whoever cared to bend his eye close enough to make it out.

He held back a smile. "And you know what the cow is saying, don't you? She says: 'Your tradition, my ass.'"

He showed me that the cow was pulling an old bullock cart and pointed out the intricately entwined figures he'd introduced in a minute scale into the body of the cart.

"This is me as a sadhu baba with folded arms," he said, pointing it out.

He ran his finger along the line of a woman's body, which I hadn't seen. Her body was ingeniously entwined as the background around the ascetic figure.

"That," he said, "is my European lady. We've been married a few decades now."

He pointed out the Indian figure wrapped in a shawl riding in the cart. "And you know what *he's* saying in response to the cow's 'Your tradition, my ass,' don't you? He is, after all, riding downwind of this methane producer. He says: 'Your progress, my gas,' he said, holding his nose for effect.

He let me hold the tiny piece of paper, while he explained his art. The miniature painting was composed of individual dots produced by the tips of variously colored ball point pens. He had spent weeks bent over this piece of paper, tap—tap—tapping individual points with the colored pens to produce the most intricate designs, a whole world in miniature.

He went quickly through his paintings, offering descriptions and explanations where needed. "This one is called, When Silence Covered the Sky. It took me six weeks." He turned the page. "This one is my erotic painting, though it is only a little erotic." It was a figureless abstract. "This one— do you see the hand beneath the foot? It is based on a mystical saying. God says: 'Where my devotee, my lover, keeps his foot, I put my hand beneath it. I follow him always, and I never leave him alone.'

"This one, all in blue, was made entirely with a single ball pen. A five rupees ball pen. It still needs some polishing."

"This one reveals the shape of my heart."

"This is Jesus Christ. One hand here. The other imagine there. There's the cross. This is the head. You must stand somewhere here and look up. If you look closely, you'll see a face in the background, giving him a kiss. In the art world of Europe, we have two Christos, or Christs. The Crucified Christ and the Triumphant Christ. This one is triumphant.

"This is my latest—of two or three years ago. I like to call it the sacred and the profane. It is not ready. Wherever there is an excess of light—I will dot it."

I couldn't help but wonder aloud, "And these are all made with tick-tick-tick…"

"I know nothing else," he said. "It takes more than just time: it requires a certain—paranormal something."

"What does?"

"This," he said, and he made once like he was tapping a pen. "To place the dot. It is not an ordinary dot. It has evolved over time, this particular method I employ.

"It is possible to penetrate the dot, to pass within it, and to come out the other side where there is an infinite picture, of which these," he said, patting his paintings, "are the slices."

He snapped his case shut and straightened his spine.

"And that, my friend, is how you should remember me. There is just one point, and the point is always the same. I call my collection: The Interior of a Dot."

I pulled my camera out from under my jacket. "May I take your photo?"

"At the moment my face is so tense," he said. "Please don't take it."

I let the camera slide back under my jacket.

"You are feeling tense?"

"This is why I am asking if you want to have a tea, so I can have a smoke. I smoke, you know."

When he saw that I wouldn't budge, he reopened his case and showed me more of his miniatures.

"Thousands upon thousands of dots," I marveled.

"It's all one dot."

"How did you come to this?

"It was 1980. In Goa."

"Were you painting before that?"

"I was doing dry brush. In 1970, when I was twenty-one, I took a boat from Bombay and went to Athens. I had no money, but I had some paintings so I sold them. Then I went to Germany, and I gave lectures on yoga. I was a Sikh and always wore a turban. My beard was almost to my navel. My accent was right. I certainly looked the part. But all I knew was what I'd read in books. I spoke in front of three hundred

American students, and two, three other places. I gave lectures on yoga in Italy and Switzerland and arrived back in Germany. I gave that whole thing up and sold newspapers in the cafés, that was in Munich, and I fell in love with a German girl, Sylvie. I lived about six years in Germany. And then I wrote a book. It is called *Sans Sylvie*. It means Without Sylvie. I have one copy at home. Then I returned to India. I lived with an English girl from Oxford and her six-year-old daughter. We lived in Goa. That's when I first came to the dot. It was 1980 in Goa. And then I left again for Paris. I lived there three years. Painting, but not making money. I've never had money. A painter needs money like anyone else, for food and for one of these," he said, fingering his jacket, which was rather threadbare. "Everybody needs to stay warm. Rupees *are* necessary. We do not deny this existential reality. Even today I have next to no money."

As if to demonstrate, he called to a beggar who was just passing by. He opened his purse and gave the beggar half his precious coins.

"It must be tough," I said as the beggar walked off, "living on the street like that."

"I don't think about such things," he said. "It's nonsense. You have a lot more to think about as well. You have your life. And I have mine. And maybe if I have God's blessing, some of it will go to him too. That's my responsibility, to be in the right place—so he can also have benefit. That is why I want to take these forty paintings and exhibit them."

"One good point is that you don't need a big space," I said. "They're so small."

"I expect them to produce a lot of money," he said, "because I know nobody else does this work. Not in the whole world. Nobody *can* do this work. There was one fellow, the first great English painter, Nicholas Hilliard. He did portraits one-and-a-half inches across. *Fantastic*! His self-portrait is a masterpiece. I'm convinced he had this technique. I'm sure of it."

"When did he paint?"

"It was the late 16th century."

"That still makes you the first to use the ball point pen!"

"Yes," he said, rocking his head as only an Indian can, "that is correct."

I took my camera out from under my jacket.

"May I take a picture of you now? You don't look tense at all. The sun's light is just right. In photography, light is the most important thing."

NICHOLAS HILLIARD, SELF PORTRAIT, 1557

"What you say is also true for painting," he said.

He told me I could take his picture. I snapped the shutter and tucked the camera back under my jacket.

"Do you know that we are really enemies," he said.

"How's that?"

"Your business, photography, ever since the late 19th century has made all the painters jobless."

"If you had to choose between knowledge and happiness," he said, "which would you choose?"

I told him happiness, and I explained why.

"Happiness," he said. "Bliss.... The divine and our relation to it was put most succinctly in India in this simple formula as old as time itself: Sat—Chit—Ananda: existence, consciousness, and bliss. We only know of our existence because we are conscious. That is what separates us from the rock. This formula tells us that the nature of this consciousness is bliss. You can take delight in existence, in the phenomenal world, or you can take delight in consciousness itself. The artistic way, the way of the spiritual man, or woman, is the delight of consciousness, at least for us human beings. If you want to take delight in existence, in the phenomenal world, you can always go and buy that in the consumer market. But an artist—a spiritual person—must live the existence of consciousness. Consciousness is light is knowledge. And bliss is just its nature."

The next line he practically sang:

> If you're in the right place,
> If you're rightly aware—
> Bliss will be there!

"We are back, my friend, to a question of *why* and *how*. The real question is not *why* I am miserable, but *how* can I be this bliss." He raised his right eyebrow. "That is, if you go after the bliss. Not knowing *how* to achieve bliss but asking *why* you are miserable: that is the work of psychology. It can probably make you better adjusted to your role in this world, it might make you less trouble for others—but it certainly will not lead you to bliss."

"To be honest, lately I've felt a little estranged, which is a sign of depression. I do not know whether I'm feeling estranged from the world, or from myself. In the end it does not matter.

"To be truthful, for the last few days I'm not feeling *so* estranged; I've come to a state where my head has been very much prominent, and not the body. My body is sixty-three years old, and it only weighs 100 pounds.

"When you walk on the street and the seven sages—your senses—are fully functioning, then you know what William James meant when he said, 'Consciousness is experienced above the neck.' And he is quite correct, in a way; but in our Indian system, it says it is by the power of the heart that the head is held high. First, the energy must rise to make the heart strong. Only then can the head be firm. And the dot requires a very still head. It must come from a still point. Do you know Aldous Huxley? Huxley talked of this still point."

I recalled the opening quote of Huxley's book *Time Must have a Stop*, some lines from Shakespeare. I asked him whether he knew these lines, for I'd memorized them years before and it somehow stuck. I recited them:

> But thought's the slave of life, and life time's fool;
> And time, that takes survey of all the world,
> Must have a stop.

I asked him if he'd read the book.

"No," he said, "but I did read *Point Counter Point.*"

He shifted on his feet and continued: "There is one of Shakespeare's sonnets that I'm rather close to, in which he speaks of Time's pencil—and, I may add, his *pupil's pen.* I've always taken it as an inspiration for my paintings."

Instead of reciting the line from the sonnet, he sort of sang it, calling out the last word:

"To give away yourself, keep yourself *still!*"

He didn't mind people turning to see what the commotion was.

"But if I'm to keep myself still and paint," he said, "the question naturally arises: *How* am I supposed to make a living? As I said, we mustn't deny the existential reality we find ourselves in. But it's certainly not easy, these days, being a painter. Not since you photographers came along. It requires us to come down off the hill every now and again with offerings for the market. Thankfully, Shakespeare gives us the answer to my question of how to live in the last line of his sonnet. He says: You must live drawn by your own sweet *skill!*"

"This," he said, bending close to my ear, "is yoga—to be drawn forward by your own sweet and innate skill. This is also the true artist's *intrinsic* motivation with which we began our conversation."

I pulled out my camera. It was time to leave. And besides, the light was fading. I asked if I could take another photo. I wanted to preserve another slice of that infinite picture.

"Yes," he said, "but my face is very serious."

I snapped the shutter.

"It's my nature," I said, "this photography."

"Writing would be OK," he said. "It is photography that is questionable. Yet I once did something similar: I went around Paris one day looking for the face of God in the people I met. And I did find one or two persons who seemed quite close."

He gave the bulge my camera made in my jacket a friendly poke.

"Maybe, sir," he said, "you are also looking for the face of God in your portraits?

We both had to get going.

"How should I remember you?" I asked.

"I already told you before: I penetrate the dot, and on the other side is an infinite picture. I paint slices of that picture; that is all. And I love God."

He turned to leave.

Then he paused.

"Maybe I speak English better than other Indians."

He laughed, turned, and disappeared in the crowd.

Amram,
Balancing on the Edge

I

When I first saw Amram I was navigating through the market in upper Dharamsala on a busy afternoon. I was in a hurry, late to meet a friend for lunch. A car was trying to squeeze past a cart whose driver was absent. I nipped between two stalls to a widening of the sidewalk, an area in front of a few shops that was clear only because no vehicles could reach it.

He was clearly a Westerner, and he was clad in a white

robe, standing alone in the middle of this little open area. With long gray hair from a balding crown and a beard to his chest, he looked ancient, wizened. Quite small and slightly stooped, with his feet planted a little too far apart, apparently in a bid to keep his balance, his arms were outstretched before him like a sleepwalker's for equilibrium. His hands trembled, and it seemed neurological. The intensity of his concentration, staring at a point on the ground before him, naturally aroused both my curiosity and my concern.

Could he be the same man I had seen in a dramatic scene a few years before? It was at the security gate to the Dalai Lama's offices and private quarters. The Dalai Lama had been giving public teachings at his temple and it was the lunch break. It is well known that the Dalai Lama gives private audiences during these breaks.

Quite a few bystanders, myself included, had gravitated to a respectful distance from the gate, guarded by both Tibetan guards and the Indian army. We were watching people—many of whom were dressed in magnificent Tibetan costume—show their credentials to the guards and pass through. A group of people exited the gate having had their audience, ceremonial white silk scarves around their necks, glowing with their encounter. We were waiting also because soon enough the mid-day break would be over and we'd be well positioned to see the Dalai Lama and his retinue of guards and monks and officials come out through the gate and return to the temple, a minute's walk away, to continue his program.

It was while watching this scene that a car had driven up to the gate, which was unusual since the whole temple-residential complex was restricted and had armed guards at the entrances. Everybody had to go through metal detectors and pat-downs. Only VIPs were allowed to bypass security by having the outer gates opened for them so they could be driven in. And what vehicles were allowed through tended to be those of upper level government representatives, often with tinted windows, or maybe an army jeep, but not a normal beat-up white taxi, of the kind that clogged the town's streets, like this one, which stopped in front of the gate.

The back door swung open and a bearded young man got out, an ascetically thin and earnest Westerner in his mid-twenties. He opened the passenger door for an old man who—like the man now before me in the market—had long straight straggly grey hair and a beard to match. The young man was quite tall and had to almost double over to put the old man's white robe-clad arm over his shoulder so he could lift him out. The old man could hardly carry his own weight.

His appearance was so striking that those around me began to speculate about who he was and what was wrong with him, whether he'd had a stroke, or had maybe been in a horrendous accident. And though he had to be held up, the old man added to the drama of the moment by propelling himself forward, seemingly drawn by an irresistible and reckless force. Someone suggested that maybe he was dying and wanted to get the blessings of His Holiness before he did so. He looked so ancient that age alone could have been enough to account for his condition. That he was a Westerner, wore a white robe with a white beard to his navel, only increased the air of mystery. He looked like a sage, as if he'd just come off a mountain.

One of the guards with a rifle slung across his back came out and put the old man's other arm over his shoulder. At the gate the young man produced their passports and explained who they were. He acted toward the old man with diffidence, as if he were escorting a revered and holy man.

They passed through the gate and that was the last I saw of either of them, though I wondered what transpired between him and the Dalai Lama and what happened to him after. There was an intensity to the scene that left an impression on me so strong that even now, some years later, I was quite certain that it was the same old man standing so uncertainly in the busy market, even though he was hunched over with his chin on his chest and I could barely see his face. Before, he had been the center of attention; now, he had about him an air of abandonment.

I watched him for a moment, to see whether he needed

assistance. But he seemed OK. A glance at my watch told me I was late to meet my friend, and I decided to pass on. His chin was on his chest and as I passed him he peered up at me through his bushy grey eyebrows. He spoke, but his words got caught in his sage-like beard.

I stopped and came closer.

"Do you speak English?" he was saying. His voice was high-pitched and shaky and his accent was American.

"Yes."

"Could you help me sit down?"

"Of course," I said.

He extended a hand toward me; it was shaking uncontrollably. Thinking he was about to fall, I latched onto both his forearms. It was difficult to judge the extent or immediacy of his extremis, nor imagine where, in the middle of the market, he could sit.

He said something, and I had to bend my ear to his beard to understand.

"Behind me," he said, indicating with a slight nod of his head, "you'll find two chairs. One has a cushion on it. Bring it here."

For the first time, he raised his chin from his chest and looked me so directly in the eye that I was taken completely off guard. I don't know how long his eyes pierced into mine, but it was so intense that for some moments I forgot the crowded market. My hands were clasped onto his forearms, feeling his rhythmically firing neurons, and I was staring into his dark brown, almost black, eyes, glowing with a strange intensity. I had to shake off the idea that he was attempting to convey something with his eyes, something unspeakable, that he was directing a force at me, an insight, perhaps; could it be something he gained by his close proximity to death?

He started swaying backward and I tightened my grip. Was I there to witness his death, there in the middle of bustling the market? Was he attempting to transfer his last thoughts, his last insights? Who the hell was he?

"Are you alright?"

"Yes," he said. "I am all right. I just have to stabilize."

His breath was shallow.

"Take hold of my hands."

I did so.

His voice was sharp, commanding. It was something of a relief. It seemed his condition had not suddenly spiraled to the worse; it was something he understood and knew how to handle. He just needed my help to 'stabilize.'

"I am going to lean back," he announced, "and you must let me."

His hands were almost sparking with neural electricity.

"Hold tight, and don't let go."

I did as instructed.

He started rocking from side to side, and leaning back to the edge of imbalance.

I tried to counter his movements, to hold him steady, clutching his hands so tightly that I feared crushing the fragile bones.

He suddenly stopped swaying and let out a moan of impatience.

"No," he said, clearly irritated. "You're not doing it correctly. You mustn't be too rigid. Let me lean back so I can stabilize, just don't let go. I am going to lean back. Let me—just don't let me crash."

He began swaying and leaning back rhythmically in a kind of crazy gyration, coming ever closer to the point of imbalance. Though his tremor was obviously neurological, it did cross my mind that there could have been some madness in it too.

It took tremendous discipline on my part, and immense trust, to allow him to teeter on the edge, to hold him steady without restraining him, to provide him the safety he needed so he could, as he said, stabilize.

And I began to get a sense of what he meant by stabilize. It seemed a subtle thing.

His chin was back on his chest, and he was staring intently into my solar plexus and his body was shaking. His entire neurological system was firing in rhythmic waves from his hands into mine, up my arms and throughout my body.

His awareness was far, far away, yet through his eyes he was concentrating his entire being on my solar plexus, all the while leaning recklessly backwards as I tread the thin line between restraining him and letting him go completely, which of course I couldn't since I was now responsible for him not smacking his skull on the ground.

The situation was so radically out of my control that it occurred to me something else might be going on, something I could not comprehend. My mind began to speculate in ways it normally wouldn't. Who was this old man with the atmosphere of decades in Central Asia, and what did he want with me? There was an intensity of the moment, as if something of great importance was about to occur, as if something subtle yet powerful might be transferred, as if time was short. Could he be an adept, a modern-day shaman or a yogi, putting himself into a trance by rhythmically rocking, attempting a transfer of consciousness? Could something have gone wrong in his psychic experiments that lead to his neurological condition? Was he trying to suck energy from me now that I couldn't possibly let go? There was an atmosphere of death about him, as if he had one foot on the other side. It was all so unlikely and beyond my control, yet so intensely real, that anything could have been happening.

He was leaning now on the very backs of his heels.

He sensed my concern, and without breaking his rhythm, he said something I couldn't hear. So I bent close to hear him, his shallow breath spacing his words and making each distinct: "To achieve balance, we must go to the very edge of imbalance."

His movements slowly became more rhythmic and centered.

"I think I'm ready," he announced.

Ready for what, I wondered. I brought my ear closer to his beard.

"You can get the chair now and bring it here."

"But can I let go of you? Can you stand without falling?"

"Give me a moment, let me become stable—OK, now you

can go and get it."

Slowly releasing my hold on his hands, I rushed for the plastic chair with the cushion. I placed it directly behind him so he could sit.

"That's not the right place for the chair," he said, again with an air of irritation. "Move it a one step to the right."

I would have thought he needed the chair directly behind him. But I did as I was told. Then I took his hands and led him to it, and turned him so he could sit.

"Move it a little to the left," he said. "No, not that much, just like this," and he indicated a hair's distance between his trembling thumb and forefinger.

I moved the chair a corresponding, almost imperceptible, nudge to the right, but it was too much. He had me move the chair but a hair's breadth left. Each time I had to help him stabilize, go behind the chair, move it, then come back and hold his hands.

The situation was both grave and absurd. It crossed my mind—though not in a very serious way—that maybe he was playing with me. On top of his neurological condition, he could still be mad.

It was as if he had been laying in wait for me. Maybe it was all part of a surrealistic sociological experimental study of the Good Samaritan, to see how far people would go with someone in distress. Maybe I was being filmed or would have to fill out a questionnaire. But no one could fake the tremble and electrical firing of the neurons.

"Now it is good," he said. "Hold my hands again and help me get positioned."

It was a painstaking process. His feet moved slowly, each shuffling step about the breadth of a pencil. He was positioning himself squarely in front of the chair. Then he told me to move the cushion a little to the left, and some back to the right, until finally he said it was right.

"I am going to fall back," he announced, "and you are going to let me. I'm going to land in this chair." He took a deep breath. "Just don't let the chair fall over."

He started shaking, and again the labored breathing and

his hands in mine pulsing, his intense stare at my solar plexus. I could feel him about to depart, as if he were entering a trance. But before he could do so, his body suddenly stiffened and he fell backwards like a board—or rather like an old gnarled log.

It seemed a wildly reckless thing to do.

My reflexes were sharp and I propped my feet against the flimsy chair's front legs so it wouldn't topple and I cushioned his freefall by holding back on his hands.

Finally he was seated!

As if I had come upon a foundering ship on the high seas and towed it safely to port, he was seated. He had asked me to help him sit down and I had done it. He was out of danger, my duties discharged. A glance at my watch told me I was so late now that the friend I was to meet for lunch might have given up on me by now.

"I'm slouching," he said.

"What?"

"I'm not sitting far enough back."

Because I had held back on his freefall and prevented him from fully crashing into the chair, his ass *had* landed something shy of the chair's back—so he *was* in fact slouching.

"You should have more trust," he said, "to let things take their own course, without interfering. This is from the great teaching of Taoism. You should have let me go. I know how to fall freely. Now you're going to have to lift me up again so I can sit properly."

"Couldn't I just scoot you back?"

"No."

I held onto his hands and moved my feet back so I could bear the weight of helping him up, but he objected.

"Put your feet directly in front of mine," he insisted, "so our toes are touching."

I hesitated, but he insisted: "I said place yourself so our feet are facing, exactly toe to toe."

That was not where I'd place my feet to brace myself and hold my center of balance when I lifted him. Why was it so important to him that our toes were touching? It was like being trapped in a strange dream. My mind started grasping at straws, imagining hidden agendas. Crazy notions of an energy transference resurfaced in my mind. With his age and his white robe, his flowing white hair and long beard to his chest, anything was possible. He was practically sparking with electricity.

To break the spell of his overwhelming presence I looked around me, to reassure myself that I was still in fact in the middle of the Dharamsala market. It was then I noticed, not ten paces away, that there was a man with a microphone speaking into a rather large Television camera perched on another man's shoulder. They were from one of the major Indian networks, shooting a report from this center of the Tibetan exile community on the recent spate of self immolations. The angle of their shot was such that my encounter with this strange old man could well be being captured in the background, adding to the surreal quality of the entire situation.

We held hands and I lifted him up to standing.

Again, I put my ear close to his beard so I could hear him.

"Now," he said, "I want you to move the chair over there, where you got it from, next to the other chair." And he indicated the shop front where I'd gotten the thing from in the first place. By now, I knew arguing would be useless and only prolong the situation.

Holding his hands until he stabilized, I then rushed the chair next to the other, then hurried back. Holding his hands, turning him around, and walking backwards, I helped him toward the chair, which was now about four paces away. The process was painstakingly slow, interrupted numerous times by his swaying motion as he brought himself to the brink of falling in order to find his balance. At one point he even lifted a leg behind him, leaned forward for balance, and started practically pirouetting on his one foot in his eternal search for balance, all the while his eyes practically staring holes into my solar plexus.

I let him fall freely into the chair this time. It took tremendous discipline on my part to release him to his fate. But I did so, and it was a success. He sat squarely in the chair, and again I felt freed from my immediate responsibility. The boat was docked. Now I could proceed to the restaurant and see whether my friend was still there. But curiosity got the better of me. I sat down in the other chair and asked whether it could have been him I saw some time ago going in for an audience with the Dalai Lama.

He mumbled into his beard. I leaned closer, and he repeated: "Would you like to see the picture?"

His trembling hand started going for the zipper of his inside vest pocket, but his fingers could not connect around the zipper pull. So he asked me to do it for him. I reached my hand into his vest, unzipped the pocket, and pulled out a laminated photo of him and the Dalai Lama touching foreheads taken on that day I'd first seen him.

"Are you Jewish," he asked as I was looking at the photo.

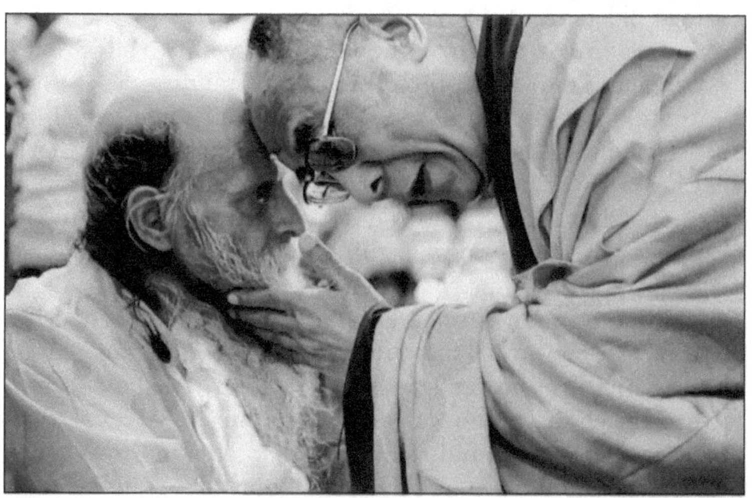

"Yes," I said, "if not by religion, then by ancestry. I come from that tribe."

"I am also Jewish," he said, "Maybe I'm the last wandering Jew. For over forty years I've been on the road; I've traveled to over one hundred countries."

He told me he was originally from New York and I told him what town I was from just outside Boston. He knew the town and used to go there: "A long time ago I had a girlfriend

for
26-8068
et
GIO ATHLETIC

from that town, we were going to be married. Her family's house was just off Route 9."

He mentioned the road and I knew it. It was odd, to say the least, to be sitting on a plastic chair in the busy Dharamsala market speaking with this peculiar—to say the least—old man about a particular obscure road in my home town, which I'd also left long ago.

I glanced at my watch, remembering my friend.

"I've got to go," I said. "I'm late for a meeting."

"I'm here every afternoon between one and five," he said. "Please. Come back."

It was somewhere between a plead and a command.

"OK," I said. "I will. What's your name?"

"Amram," he said, "Amram: he was the father of Moses."

"The father of Moses?"

"Yes. That is my name."

And so I left him alone on his chair in the middle of the market, confident that he'd freefall into his next situation.

When I reached the restaurant, my friend was just leaving, so we went back in and I told him of my encounter. My nerves still felt the electric pulse from Amram's neuronal firings. It took some days for it to go away.

II

A few weeks later I was back in Dharamsala and met up with the same friend I had had lunch with. We'll call him David, and he had a story for me.

A few days after we'd last met he had been going by Amram's corner in the afternoon and there he was just as I'd described. Amram was sitting on the same plastic chair with a cushion on it in front of the shop; there was an empty seat next to him. David was curious, so approached Amram and was invited to sit down. They hadn't been talking long before Amram announced that he had to urinate and that David would have to help. David had worked with disabled people, and while astounded by the audacity of Amram's placing himself at the mercy of passersby, he was also able to handle Amram's request.

He had held both of Amram's hands, stood him up, and shuffled with him ("Just as you described!") to the end of the narrow line of shops, where a rusted spiral staircase and a tree were sandwiched between buildings. Lest you think it was tucked away, it wasn't: it was right on the street within sight of every passerby. Amram had hidden there a plastic water bottle with the top cut off. David had to unzip Amram's fly, pull out his member, position the plastic bottle, and help him pee.

"I was willing to do it," David said, laughing, "but it was all pretty intense."

Later that afternoon I went to Amram's corner. The two chairs were set in the middle of the sidewalk, but they were empty. I saw the spiral staircase and the tree between shops. A blond-haired woman was slowly backing away from the tree. At first all I could see was her back, and that she was stooped over; then I saw that she was leading Amram. I was both relieved that this duty wouldn't fall to me and fascinated to see he had found a woman to assist.

I hung back at a distance from the empty chairs, no doubt their destination. The woman was quite tall and had to bend almost double to hold his hands in hers and to put her ear to his beard in order to hear him and to coax him along.

From time to time they stopped, and holding his hands in hers she made wide arcing movements with her arms. It looked like the slow-motion movements of a strange and primitive dance, but actually she was stretching his limbs, loosening his cramping muscles, performing physical therapy right there in the middle of the Dharamsala market. Typical of the mad swirl of India, no one paid them any mind.

She sat him in the chair and sat next to him. When I came over she immediately started explaining to him that she had to go. I was clearly opening the window for her departure, since she wouldn't be leaving him alone.

Once she was gone, he lifted his chin from his chest, which took an effort, looked at me with no discernible sign of recognition, and asked in a businesslike manner, almost as if he were a bureaucrat and I'd entered his office, "How do you spell your name?"

"First name or last?" I remembered how particular he was.

"First."

I spelled Thomas.

"Have we met before?" he asked.

"About two weeks ago, at this very spot. You told me you've been traveling forty years."

"For forty years I've been on the road without a break," he said, almost mechanically, as if it was a practiced statement that he gives out with regularity.

"What made you keep going all those forty years?"

"I was on a spiritual path, searching for myself. One takes many wrong turns. I had to go that far to find out it was inside me all along. I spent 12 years in a caravan, what's called a motor home in the States. For 12 years I went to all fifty United States, Canada, and Mexico. I also lived in Jerusalem for 10 years. Now I've been eighteen years in India. My main purpose has been meeting saints and sages and going to holy places.

"Once I met a 500-year-old saint. That was at the Kumbh Mela, the holy gathering of sages every twelve years where the Ganges and Jamuna rivers meet. When I met him I cried for an hour. I could not stop.

"The scriptures of India tell stories of people becoming enlightened by another person through a single look, or a solitary word. They even say it can be conveyed through touch. Even to touch the hem of their robe."

He looked more intently into my eyes, and again I had this uncomfortable feeling, like he was boring into me. I recalled the energy that had pulsed through his hands and into mine.

"There are three qualities necessary to gain the most from such encounters," Amram said. "Surrender, Serenity, and—I can't remember, but there is one more."

"I guess the trick is finding the third one," I laughed.

"*Faith*," he said. "That's it: surrender, sincerity, and faith. You must surrender to what is greater, have sincerity in your search, and faith in the entire enterprise. Faith not in the strictly religious sense, but just the belief that it's possible. That openness will allow for it."

Amram was silent a moment. Then he changed the subject.

"Do you know Sri Aurobindo and The Mother?" He was referring to one of India's great spiritual leaders of the 20th century and his French collaborator.

"Yes."

"Did you know that The Mother was Jewish, and that she built the largest ashram in India?"

"No, I didn't know that."

"Are you Jewish?"

"You asked me that last time. Yes, I am, at least by birth."

"Have you heard of the lost Jews of Tibet? No? Well there are also many Jews in India."

I told him I had heard of the Jews of Cochin, in South India.

"They're only the most famous," he said. "There are six different settlements of Jews in India. I've researched this quite extensively. I've written a manuscript about it. If you come tomorrow I will bring it. I'm trying to raise funds."

I told him I had to leave now, but that I'd come back to see the manuscript.

"Tomorrow is my birthday," he said. "I will be sixty years old tomorrow."

I had guessed he was around ninety.

"My name is Amram," he said. "Amram was the father of Moses."

"Yes, you told me."

"Thomas," he said, "that's not a Jewish name."

"My parents aren't religious, maybe that's why."

"I'm much the same," he said. "I'm a universal."

III

When I arrived late the next afternoon, Amram's birthday, he was sitting on his cushioned plastic chair holding court. In addition to the other chair, there were two low bamboo stools.

A couple who had been standing and talking with him were just leaving. The blond-haired woman from the day before was sitting on the chair to his right, and a young man with a yarmulke and straight black hair flopping over his ears was occupying the first stool to his left. I wished Amram a happy birthday and sat on the other stool.

Amram was showing a large loose-leaf binder to the young man, who was from Israel and didn't speak English well. Amram was giving a presentation by going through the pages of his folder, and it was clear he'd given this talk many times before. It came round to a request for funds.

In the front was a letter from Ram Das, the ex-Harvard professor (born as Richard Alpert and raised in my home town) who turned on with Timothy Leary in the '60s, came to India, and became something of a Western holy man, authoring many books along the way and founding numerous charitable organizations. The letter was in support of Amram and his Star of the East Foundation headquartered, so the stationery said, on Fifth Avenue, New York (an address and suite number that a subsequent Internet search proved to be the suite used by a 'virtual office and mail forwarding service,' which allows any number of businesses and entities to use the same 'prestigious' Fifth Avenue address and have their mail forwarded anywhere in the world. My Internet search revealed that this suite is presently the address of a Hollywood production service, an accident lawyer, an artist, and a literary agent, among others).

Amram had the blond-haired woman read out part of the letter: "Bringing to the world consciousness the history and plight of the Indian Jewish community is a worthy project

... such attention can bring assistance in strengthening and preserving their rituals and traditions and in caring for their poor and destitute. Knowledge of the Jewish community in India should bring pride to Jews throughout the world. May the work of the Star of the East Foundation, motivated as it is by love, go forward with strength and find favor and support in the hearts of many."

There were other letters too, from apparently famous scholarly rabbis, singing rabbis, rabbis Amram was surprised I'd never heard of, editors of Jewish newspapers in New York, Tel Aviv, and Jerusalem, as well as all manner of leaders of Jewish organizations—all in support of Amram and the work of his foundation.

In this loose-leaf binder was his foundation's proposed budget, a huge thing with pages of line items. Apart from a travel budget and daily allowance for food and lodging, airplane tickets and the like, he had a budget for camera equipment, which included seven cameras and an astounding $2,714 for film. How strange, in this world of digital cameras. Then I noticed the letters and the budget were all dated from the mid 1980s.

He turned to a photograph of the brass plaque from a donation box at a synagogue, I believe in Mumbai. Written on the plaque in Hebrew, Hindi, and English was, "Charity De-

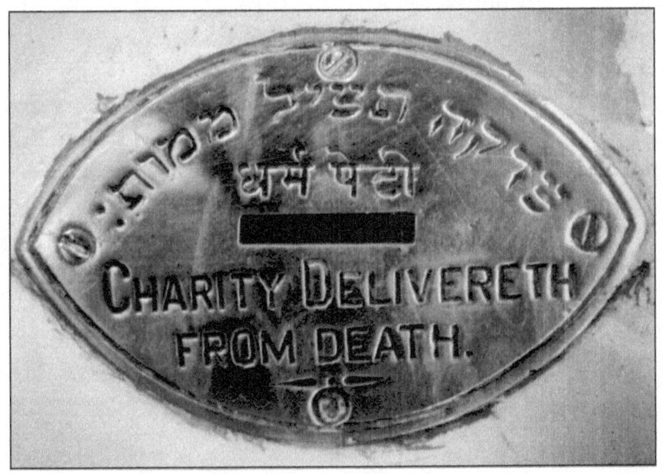

livereth From Death."

"I'm looking for funders for my project," Amram told the Israeli guy, "but first I must get better. I've found a doctor in the Philippines who can help me."

The Israeli guy's English wasn't good enough for him to grasp much of what Amram was saying.

The blond-haired woman explained, I think to me more than to the Israeli guy: "You know, these psychic surgeons. He explained to me they also call them bare-hand surgeons. They claim to reach into people's bodies with their bare hands and take out disease. He knows of one in the Philippines that someone told him could cure his neurological condition."

She gave me a doubtful look over Amram's head.

"That's right," Amram said, "I need $3,000 to go there, and that is what I'm raising funds for now. Then I can get back to my project."

The Israeli guy was obviously a bit confused. "What exactly the money is for?" he asked.

"To go to the Philippines."

The Israeli guy said: "My friend Daniel speaks English very good. We are many Israelis here. If you let, I take this notebook and he read to us all. He translate, and maybe we help."

"You may not take this notebook anywhere," Amram said curtly. "I have never let anyone take the notebook. This is my only copy. Your friends must come here: I'm here between one and five every afternoon."

"OK, I tell my friends," the Israeli said. "How many groups of Jews you say are in India?" He had already lost the details he would have to narrate to his friends.

"There are six communities, in all parts of the country. The oldest seems to be the one in India's far east, in Mizoram, in the jungles on the Burmese border. I've been there. It is a very remote area."

I asked Amram how a group of Jews made it there.

"It was 400 BC, after the destruction of the first temple. They came by way of China. They are from the Menashe tribe; Menashe was the son of Joseph, who was one of the twelve sons of Jacob. They are from the lost tribe of Israel."

The Israeli guy said he'd heard of the Menashe, and that many had recently come back to Israel.

"That's right," Amram said. "Over a thousand have emigrated."

He went on to explain the controversy surrounding the emigration of the Menashe Jews from the jungles of Mizoram. Apparently their cause has been championed within Israel by some ultra-conservative rabbis who are also finding accommodation for them in brand new housing—in newly built settlements on Palestinian land. It isn't easy to find people within Israel willing to live on the front lines.

"I have to go," the Israeli guy said. "I must go pray with the others."

"Look," Amram said before the guy could leave his seat. "I have to raise money."

"Right," the Israeli guy said, "three hundred dollars."

"Three thousand."

"OK. I ask my friends. If I can take this book, it is very good to help you."

"Anyone can come here and talk to me," Amram said.

"OK. I send my friends here. Tell again: What do you really need money for?"

"To be cured," Amram said, testily. "To go to the Philippines, to stay in the Philippines, and to come back from the Philippines."

"How long do you want to stay there?"

"A couple of months."

"Yeah, that doesn't sound like so much. I think maybe I can do something..."

Amram's face lit.

The blond-haired woman intervened. "Do you really think you can? Because to raise hopes—"

"I will have my friend Daniel come and look," he said. "He can read English."

He stood up. "Good birthday to you, Mr. Amram, but I must go."

When he left, the blond-haired woman took the loose-leaf

binder from Amram and handed it to me. She put a hand on Amram's shoulder. "Shouldn't we stretch?"

"Thomas," Amram said, "can you wait? Can you *please* wait?"

"Yes," I said, "I'll just look through this till you come back."

"No!" he exclaimed. "Don't look at it. Wait until I come back."

"But how will I restrain myself," I said laughing. "I won't harm it. Is it OK if I just flip through it until you come back?"

"No!"

"OK. OK. Don't worry. I won't."

"There's a reason."

I closed the book.

"I'll be right back," he said. "I'm taking a stretch."

"We'll just walk a little bit," the blond-haired woman said, positioning herself in front of Amram's chair. She put her feet so she was toe to toe with him and helped him up. They shuffled across the sidewalk, stopping now and again for her to stretch his arms in wide, wing-like gyrations. Her ear was bent to Amram's beard and they were having an intense discussion.

While they were gone a young man from England came to wish Amram a happy birthday. His name was Steven. I offered him a stool and while we watched Amram and the woman cross and recross the space in front of the shops, he told me how he first met Amram, a few months earlier.

This was Steven's first trip to India and he was touring around. Dharamsala was just one place on his itinerary. He was eating alone one evening in a cheap noodle house and as he was leaving he passed by where Amram was sitting and Amram made a request quite similar to the request he first made of me. He asked the young man to help him stand up, which of course he did. While they were standing there— and, I'm sure, while Steven helped him 'stabilize'—Amram offered to tell the young man some of what he'd learned in a lifetime of journeying. He said he had traveled to many holy places and met many holy men.

Steven, who came to India, and especially to Dharamsala,

for the reasons many young Westerners do, felt that when an old sage pops up under such conditions and offers spiritual advice, especially in perfect English, you don't pass it by. They fell into conversation and ended up sitting back down for a cup of tea.

Amram told Steven he'd once been the disciple of an elderly sage from South India, now long dead, who had revived an ancient Hindu tradition of absorbing spiritual energy directly from the rising sun. His method was to wake up before sunrise every day and stare at the sun from the moment its rim first peeks over the horizon until it launches itself into the sky. Staring at the sun while it thus crossed the horizon would purportedly relieve all mental disturbance and sharpen the mind itself.

Amram then lowered his voice and avowed in a confidential tone that if one were to follow the teaching further one could live entirely on this solar energy. One could forsake all food and live on nothing but the nourishment of the rising sun. This was called a solar fast. After six months you would be free from all illness; and after nine you would triumph over hunger. In a whisper, Amram told him that in ancient times sages used this method to triumph over death itself.

The young Englishman felt like he was living a page out of *The Autobiography of a Yogi.*

Amram then explained to Steven that he was suffering from Parkinson's Disease and that he had refused Western medicine and had been living in Dharamsala for over a year. His immediate problem was that none of the hotels or paying guest establishments would give him a room. Apparently, they were all afraid he would die overnight and they'd have to deal with both the police and the corpse. They must have also realized that even if he didn't die he could not possibly take care of himself.

The taxi and rickshaw drivers in town all knew Amram as well, and none of them would give him a ride. They were afraid that once he got into their vehicle he'd never get out.

Amram explained to Steven that there were still a few hotels that would let him stay if someone was with him, and he asked whether Steven would agree to share a room. Steven agreed enthusiastically.

"I felt like I was walking in a dream," Steven told me. "I was going to share a room with a sage!"

Amram had his bag with him, and they moved immediately into a double room. One can only wonder at Amram's reckless daring—his freefall into circumstance—it being evening, the night being cold, his condition, and having nowhere to stay.

That night the young Englishman realized what he had gotten into. Amram needed help, as he said, "with *everything*." During the days the Englishman would help Amram around the town and they would eat at dumpling shops and other cheap dives. Somehow, Amram always heard about live music and jam sessions at one restaurant or another. They would go in the evenings to hear jazz and rehearsing Tibetan rock bands. The Englishman played the didgeridoo, which he played at whatever ad hoc jam session was happening. Amram sat in his chair and dozed.

"We were quite a pair," Steven told me, "but I quickly began to wonder how to get out of it. I was his nurse 24/7. He had to get up many times at night and I had to help him with it. After a few days it was too much and I got into a nervous state. I couldn't sleep. I liked Amram, and it felt right to help him—but it was just too much. I couldn't do it. If I'd stayed on much longer I'd have become resentful.

"Sometimes I wanted to take Amram by his shoulders and shake him. How could he have put himself into this situation? How would he ever leave? Why didn't he contact his embassy and go back home and get care from professionals? He refused all Western medicine. He was taking Tibetan medicine, which I don't think is equipped for Parkinson's. He had been on the road for forty years. For forty years he was wandering the planet, looking for freedom, that's what he told me. He had his freedom, but no one to care for him—except me!"

Steven's eyes followed Amram and the blond-haired woman shuffling back and forth, stopping now and again so she could swing his arms in large gyrating circles.

"When Amram was around twenty," Steven said, "he had

a girlfriend who wanted to marry him."

It must have been that girl from my home town.

He continued: "Amram told me about it. It was three in the morning and I had just helped him to the bathroom. Amram was sitting on the edge of his bed hunched over, dejected.

"'I should have done it,' he said.

"I asked him what he should have done.

"'Married her,' he said."

I asked Steven about Amram trying to raise money to go to the Philippines and how he afforded to live.

"He must have some money," Steven said. "His parents had plenty. When he was young they gave him a monthly allowance. That allowed him to travel. And when they died, he got another chunk, which must be reaching its end. He always paid his own way for the room and our meals. I think it's this trip to the Philippines that's beyond his budget, and he's convinced it is the only thing that will save him."

"How did you ever leave him?" I asked.

"It quickly got to the point where I just couldn't take it. It must have been after about a week. Somehow I convinced the woman who ran the hotel to let him stay by himself. I continued on to Rishikesh. I only returned here just yesterday and heard it was Amram's birthday. I've brought him something."

"How did it feel, leaving him."

"Bad. But I would have gotten angry, the way he had thrust me into it. I felt compassion for him. I felt sorry for him. I even wanted to help him. But I'm just not a nurse. That's not what I came to India for. So I just couldn't do it. After I left he did get help. Now he pays someone to take care of him. So I guess he's got enough money for that. That's her, over there."

He indicated a woman who had just joined Amram and the blond-haired woman, a stout local woman with short dark hair.

"Her name is Rosie and she is a beautician on the Jogi-wara Road."

The three of them shuffled over and they sat Amram down.

It seemed the blond-haired woman had agreed with Rosie to stay until Rosie returned. She excused herself and left.

Steven gave Amram his birthday present, which Amram said he would open later. Then Steven told Amram he had to go, but that he'd come back at sunset and take him out to dinner at one of the places they used to go.

Although Rosie was being paid to look after him, she too clearly didn't want to be there. She sat on the edge of her stool, wiry and nervous. Then she got up.

"I've got to go. You talk to him till I get back."

"I can't stay long," I said, giving her what I hoped she'd recognize as a significant look. I didn't want her to just disappear.

"It's OK," Rosie said. "However long you stay, no problem."

"Come back in ten minutes," Amram said.

"Yeah, yeah. I come back don't worry," she said over her shoulder.

Amram had the notebook on his lap.

"This is a project I'm working on," he said, wasting no time. "Right now I am raising money."

He'd been raising this money since the mid 1980s. He seemed to have forgotten that I'd just heard all about it with the Israeli guy.

"It's about the Jewish cultural heritage of India," he plowed on, "and I'd like to show it to you."

"Just to make it clear," I said, "I have no extra money to speak of and I won't be able to donate to your cause." It felt harsh saying it like that, but I didn't want false expectations. And besides, it would not feel right contributing to his trip to a bare-handed surgeon in the Philippine jungle.

Though he heard me, perhaps he didn't believe it. He ploughed on, flipping through the pages.

"This is a picture of a synagogue outside Mumbai," he said. "Look how they have to take their shoes off before entering, just like in an Indian temple. It shows how they have assimilated. This one is of the two-hundredth anniversary of the synagogue in Mumbai. Here's an article, *The Lost Jews of India*, from an Indian magazine. At this place they believe

the prophet Elisha ascended to Heaven. This man was the
poet laureate of India. He was an Indian Jew. This one's a
judge on the Indian Supreme Court. He's also an Indian Jew.
This is David Sassoon a most famous Indian Jew of the past,
a very wealthy man who built synagogues in Mumbai, Pune,
and Calcutta. At that time opium was legal and he was an
opium trader with China. This one is a synagogue for Indian
Jews in New York City. This is an Indi-
an postage stamp commemorating four
hundred years of the Cochin synagogue,
1568-1968."

"What exactly is the work of the
foundation?" I asked.

"It is to write a book. Some have
written about this community or that,
but it is my intention to put together a
book about all the Jewish communities
in India. So far, I've only done some research. I've never com-
pleted it."

"And I see here you were the executive director of Star of
the East International—"

"Yes, it is true."

He flipped further through the pages, "This is a letter
in support of the foundation from the famous singing rabbi
Shlomo Carlebach. Have you ever heard of him?

"Who?"

"He's a most famous rabbi."

"I don't know many rabbis."

"He was international. He wrote two thousand Hebrew
songs. They are known by most Israelis. Here's an article
about him: *The Yiddish Pied Piper*. Here's another article:
Jewish India. This photo was taken at the 200th anniversary
of the synagogue in Mumbai. That's me in the center."

He clearly stood out, a few decades younger, amongst the
dark-skinned rabbis of Mumbai.

When I told him I had to go, he asked for help calling Rosie. I told him she had promised to be right back, but he knew
her, and that she wouldn't come back unless called.

He had me reach into his inner vest pocket to pull out his phone.

"I've lived in India for 18 years," he said, forgetting I'd heard it all before. "And I lived ten in Israel, and in a motor caravan in the USA and Canada for twelve. I've been traveling for the last forty years—to over one hundred countries. And today is my birthday."

He was obviously in a reflective mood.

"And now you are sixty."

"Most people think I'm a hundred."

Though I had first guessed early nineties, I didn't tell him.

He was silent a moment.

"There is a doctor in the Philippines," he said. "Listen to this story."

"But I do have to be going."

"Could you *please* listen?"

"Maybe we should call Rosie first."

He told me how to open his phone and call her, and when she answered I held the phone to his beard. He told her to come. Then he asked me to wait until she did so.

Rosie must have been just around the corner, for she was there in a matter of seconds.

"I've got to go," I said.

"If you want to donate to this cause, I could give you my address."

"OK," I said, "but I've really got to go."

"I need the money. It is very important. If you know anybody—"

I never saw Amram again, though I did hear that he stayed on almost two more years in Dharamsala before being repatriated to the States. Nobody has heard from him since.

The last thing I told Amram was this: "I'll tell people about you, that's all I can do."

Now I have done that.

THE TUNNELS OF THE CREATOR

BRAHMA

In the heart of South India there is a mountain that rises like a solitary cone from the endless plain of jungle. Geologists tell us this anomaly on an otherwise flat plain is an ancient and extinct volcano formed where a tunnel of magma from the earth's mantle broke the surface before dinosaurs roamed the earth, even before the Indian tectonic plate hit the Eurasian. Being the only mountain within many days march, it has been considered sacred for at least three millennia. And because there are numerous caves hidden on its steep slopes it is perhaps inevitable, it being India, that it has always attracted holy men, some of whom have, over the centuries and according to legend, attained high levels of realization.

A huge temple complex stands like a fortress at the western edge of the mountain where the steep slope meets the flat plain; it dedicated to Shiva Nataraja, the dancing Shiva. The great walled complex is so old scholars still dispute its true age. It is well documented that on the site of the great walled complex, temples of great antiquity were built over temples of even greater antiquity.

One could say the temple's origins go so far back that they are clothed in the mythic.

This ornately carved stone temple complex, ringed by a high stone battlement with heavily fortified gates, was mentioned in the most ancient of Hindu texts. The main temple, rising to 234 feet, is visible for miles around. History books are not needed to know the temple's age; the deep ruts worn by barefoot worshippers in the stone-flagged courtyards and in the portals of shrines attests to the temple's great antiquity.

On the opposite side of the mountain, exactly due east, there is to this day another temple, smaller and less assuming, a place where a few sadhus might live, those who maintain the fire and smear themselves with ash. The two temples are believed to be of the same antiquity, and the link between them is so ancient that a persistent belief among the locals, handed down from generation to generation, speaks of a secret network of tunnels passing beneath the mountain, linking the two.

As with other holy sites of tremendous antiquity, the mountain and its surrounding temples have gone through long periods of both acclaim and insignificance, times when the power of the holy mountain was known throughout India, interspersed with times when its sacred power was known only to those in its environs, who preserved the secret knowledge and kept its history alive for future generations.

India is dotted with great holy sites. Few are known at any one time; the others lie in a state of dormancy, the fires of the tradition kept alive sometimes by a single sadhu passing it on until time itself ripens for its influence to spread and be known by many.

In traditional Indian cosmology and historical conception, time and its passage is so vast that it is reckoned in great ages and eons, *yugas* and *kalpas*, and other units of time inconceivable to creatures who dwell on the earth for less than a century. The Indian conception of time begins with Brahma, the creator god. He is depicted lying on the coils of the cosmic serpent, who is floating upon the great milky ocean of existence. Brahma lies on the serpent and he dreams. He dreams our world. One day for Brahma is equal to a thousand *Mahayugas,* or great ages, each of which is comprised of 4,320,000 of our years. And his nights are just as long. All of recorded history is but a blinking of his eye. This is meant quite literally. In the Indian conception, time has an almost infinite dimension, which repeats itself through the passing of the four great ages the universe goes through, again and again. Within this framework, every holy place has its day of ascendancy, or can lie in obscurity for all of recorded history, which—in this widest of views—flashes by in a twinkle.

Having once been a great spiritual center, the mountain with its temple complex at its base has over the course of the last few centuries fallen into obscurity. Many of the holy places of India have withdrawn, so to speak, into themselves, starting with the influence of the British and now with the modernization that is sweeping the subcontinent. They go underground to protect their light so they can shine for a future age, something like hot embers covered in ash to preserve the fire till morning. It is still unknown whether India might now be hurling too rapidly into the grand technological future for the mountain's power to be preserved. Everything does come and go. To date, the mountain still attracts yogis and sages of many persuasions. They live in the many caves that lie hidden on its slopes.

One recent visitor to the mountain and the temple complex was Greg Prichard, an English scholar of ancient Hindu sacred geography who was trained at Oxford under the famed Sanskritist Dr. Osborne. He climbed the mountain and visited the huge walled-in temple complex dedicated to the dancing Shiva. He even went to the lesser temple on the mountain's opposite side. He had been interested in the temple complex for quite some time. Initially, his investigations centered on the mystery surrounding the temple complex's main anomaly, the huge stone rampart with which it is surrounded. While the walled temple complex was mentioned in early Hindu texts, nothing of what is known of the historical conditions of the area would warrant such a defensive wall, so disproportionate to those found around any other structure in the whole of south India.

In the course of his investigations, Greg Prichard had recently unearthed some textual evidence that, if true, would cause quite a stir among his fellow Sanskritists and people in Oriental Studies. A discovery of this magnitude would give him a lasting name. The text suggested the temple complex was not originally dedicated to Shiva, but was a major center for the worship of Brahma, the Hindu god of creation. Its significance, if it were true, would be tremendous: it would be by far the largest known historical temple dedicated to Brahma in all of India and would prove the temple complex to be of a tremendous antiquity.

As is true for many creator gods in world mythology, Brahma is rather aloof—and has been for a very long time. Creators tend to give form to the world and put it in motion while leaving it to others to rule and lord over. In Hindu mythology, Brahma gave birth to those who gave birth to the human race, so he is twice removed. Having been there 'at the beginning,' when the universe was called into being, the creator belongs to a former time and does not preside over events of the day. That is the work of the other gods, Shiva, Krishna, Ganesh, Lakshmi, and Saraswati, to name but a few. These are the gods with temples, shrines, sculptures and paintings dedicated to them across the Hindu world. There are also temples and shrines to the innumerable local gods and devis. You find them by springs, in villages, and at the base of venerable trees, places that are held sacred in each unique corner of the Hindu world.

Even with this profusion of sacred sites, only rarely do you find temples dedicated to Brahma, the creator. In all of present-day India, there is only one major temple dedicated to Brahma (in Pushkar), and while one finds the occasional sculpture or shrine dedicated to him within other temples, there are, apart from Pushkar, only a handful of smaller temples that could rightly be called Brahma temples. In Hinduism the sacred splinters into a myriad of forms, which are then worshiped. In all that profusion, few Hindus, if any, consider themselves worshippers of the creator, Brahma. It is practically unheard of.

Being a scholar, Greg Prichard's objects of study were primarily historical texts obscure enough to be found only in the great libraries of Oriental studies, now mostly in European universities and in archives in Calcutta, Delhi, and Banaras. His discipline tended to be dominated by scholars who relied only on texts, on the assumption that the history they were investigating was so distant that nothing useful could be gained by speaking with the living denizens of the places they studied. Max Muller, the great 19th century German Orientalist who produced the seminal translations of the Sacred Books of the East, never once set foot in India. The only time most of Greg's colleagues left their desks and libraries for the field was when they thought the architecture or artifacts—sculptures, paintings, and the like—could offer clues to the matters they were investigating. While stones could sometimes speak, what could local inhabitants, so often uneducated, possibly know of ancient history?

Greg Prichard traveled to the temple complex in south India because he wanted to see the place he was reading about. It was more to satisfy his sense of adventure and perhaps to produce a few photographs useful for his publications, rather than out of any expectation that his journey would yield useful evidence. The temple had been well documented photographically by the Archeological Survey of India, and apart from the anomalous stone rampart, the temples within the complex had been constructed and reconstructed on top of existing temples so many times that he was certain any physical evidence of Brahma worship at the site would long ago have been covered over.

While visiting the temple complex he heard of the yogis, sadhus, and sages who lived on the mountain, some of whom were said to be quite mad. There was one, however, renowned for having spontaneously attained a full state of realization at a very early age. He had been living in various caves on the mountain for almost thirty years. Greg heard that having lived for years as a recluse, driving away anyone who appeared at the mouth of his cave, this sage was now willing to speak with visitors. His clear and simple vision, which he expressed with an almost scientific precision, was beginning to attract the attention of less theologically minded people, those for whom a clear, rational approach was not opposed to the spiritual path—all of which intrigued Greg Prichard.

Greg hiked up the mountain along a trail that was well worn by countless pilgrims. Halfway up he thought he wouldn't make it. The South Indian sun beat down so hard that his head spun. When he stood on the summit he swore never to climb the mountain again during the day. That's why, when he heard of the sage and that his cave was just on the other side of the summit, he decided to climb at night, on the night of the full moon, when his way would be lit and it would be cooler.

He was given grave warnings by the locals not to climb the holy mountain by night. When he asked them why, he was told—with the forthrightness of someone warning an unsuspecting foreign tourist not to pass through an American slum after dark—that there were demons who roam the mountain at night, some of them sticking would-be trespassers with thorns, entrapping them, and causing them to bleed to death.

Being of a rational turn of mind, his only fears concerned the feral dogs that sometimes roamed in packs on the lower reaches of the mountain; he was not concerned with local superstition.

Successfully penetrating the outer reaches of the mountain without encountering a single dog, he was following the path he had taken by day to the mountain's summit when he lost his way in the darkness and missed the trail. It was then he noticed that the bushes, which had shed their leaves for the dry season, had huge straight thorns and that he was standing in a little clearing of no more than three paces in any direction. He supposed that because by day the sun shone into the clearing, the bushes all grew in and with them their thorns, which even by the light of the moon and stars he could see were all pointing menacingly toward him. He must have slipped into this clearing along the line of the thorns, but now that he was in, there was no obvious way out. While this didn't scare him at first—it was more a silly inconvenience—he tried pulling back a branch so he could slip through. But he found the branches surprisingly stiff. It was then he felt his first wave of fear, the fear of having entered a trap.

Systematically examining his periphery, he found the weakening in the circle, a place where, if he held a particular branch with his foot and held another branch back with his hand, he could just slip through and leave the whole little inconvenience behind. He succeeded in catching the low branch with his left foot and held it down. Then he leaned forward and held the other branch back with his right hand just enough that he could jump through. But by leaning forward, a twig attached to the branch he was holding with his foot sprang loose and his ankle was pricked with the tip of a thorn. He flinched and lost his foothold on the entire branch, which sprang up, causing his hand to lose hold of the other branch, and with a suddenness that seemed to preclude the passage of time he found himself hemmed in from all sides by large straight thorns that would not allow him to make the slightest movement. No matter which way he moved, a thorn was there to pierce his flesh. He couldn't even move a hand. As it were, little drops of blood were forming from innumerable places where the tip of a thorn met his flesh. He quickly realized there was no possibility of struggle, let alone escape.

He spent a hellish night contemplating a dreadful end until he was released in the morning by a woman herding goats.

Though shaken, he was still determined to meet the sage. So he continued up the mountain, reflecting on how someone with a modern sensibility (for whom it is clear from the start that demons do not exist and can hold nobody hostage for a night on an extinct volcano) might too easily dismiss as fantasy that which has a basis in reality. His experience was just strange enough, and had left him sufficiently unhinged, that it didn't immediately spur him to the conclusion he would have made under other circumstances: namely that on the mountain grew a particularly nasty bush that the unsuspecting nighttime wanderer can easily get entangled in, sometimes with mortal consequences, and this having been the case for a long, long time, this bush was then personified by an active primitive imagination into a demon. For the first time in his life, Greg Prichard mulled over the reality of demons.

When he met the sage, he was surprised to see a man with neither long hair nor beard. His skin was not smeared in ashes and he was not wearing a loin cloth. His cave had the fastidious cleanliness reflective of a well ordered mind.

On his side, the sage was surprised to have a visitor so soon after sunrise. Greg Prichard told the sage how despite warnings he had climbed the mountain at night. He told him of his encounter. Then he asked the sage, renowned for his great clarity, what to make of it.

The sage used the opportunity to make a point about the nature of reality. For under careful questioning he vociferously refused to say outright that the demon did not exist. Rather, he said it was the wrong question. He insisted that the demon had no more or less intrinsic reality than the bush. It was clear from how he said this that he was not lending reality to the demon as much as undermining the notion of reality Greg attributed to the bush. Upon being pressed to state the difference between dream and waking reality, the sage answered with a single word: duration. His point was that what we call reality, the concrete 'things' of shared awareness, and what we call fantasy—illusion, imagination, or even dream—are all of the same stuff, and that that stuff is consciousness itself.

"You can think of a friend who is far away or you can think of an imaginary being," the sage said. "Is the thought of your friend more 'real' than the thought of that being? Aren't they both just images and thoughts; aren't both objects of consciousness, and therefore of the same 'stuff'? Wouldn't it be the same if you think of a bush or a demon?"

He then made a statement, deceptive in its directness: "Coming to the understanding is very simple," he said. "Stop confusing the world as being comprised of individual *things*."

This statement caused a barrage of useless questions to arise in Greg Prichard's mind, some of which he directed toward the sage, who responded with a profound silence. It was by means of this silence, which not a single intellectual thought could penetrate, that the sage knew he would be most likely to communicate the understanding.

After a prolonged period of silence, Greg Prichard asked the sage questions related to his scholarly inquiry about the temples and the mountain. The sage revealed that when he was young he used to have visions when living in one particularly deep cave on the mountain's north side, a cave from which he said he could hear the earth's deep rumblings. In his visions he saw a vast network of ancient tunnels within the mountain, linking the two surrounding temples. He could say neither where the entrance to these tunnels were, nor why they were there. Yet often when he went into a deep state of meditation in this particular cave, he would have a powerful and realistic vision, as if he could see into the rock and perceive the tunnels directly. He even described the odd stones with which the tunnels were lined and the way they branched and merged in the depths of the earth.

Since the tunnels of his vision were as real as his experience of the cave upon awakening, he used to ponder their reality, not only asking himself whether there really were tunnels beneath the mountain connecting the temples, but asking the more fundamental questions of reality and illusion. He explained that these contemplations served as the wedge that opened his way to the understanding. He assumed from the outset that if there were tunnels, he would never find them. Therefore he left aside the question of the tunnels' 'reality'; this left him free to pursue the question of the reality not of objects, but of experience. And this provided the key. His visions were so lifelike that he found it impossible to say they were any less 'real' than his experience of the cave when he awoke.

As Greg walked back down the mountain, cautious of the thorn bushes and thankful the trail was clear in the bright sun, not even minding the tremendous heat, he thought of what the sage had said. While he couldn't go as far as the sage in using his experience to question the fundamental nature of reality, he couldn't help linking the 'reality' of the thorn-wielding demon with the underground tunnels. If the one had proved to have a basis in reality, why not the other? The demon's basis in 'reality' had been the very real bushes with which the mountain was covered. Couldn't the unusual rampart surrounding the temple complex provide a clue? Couldn't the defensive posture that those thick stone walls implied, themselves imply a network of underground tunnels, perhaps as some form of escape?

Greg Prichard went back to the temples along the mountain's base. With a new respect for local lore borne of his experience with the 'demon,' he asked villagers and the *pujaris*, or priests, what they knew of the temples' origin. He was not surprised when more than one person mentioned underground passageways, a theme not uncommon for holy sites anywhere in the world. Ordinarily one can dismiss the vast majority of such claims: underground passageways are an archetypal theme in sacred geography and myth, and as such are usually traceable to an unconscious projection of the mysterious into the great Underground Unknown, rather than to three-dimensional passageways. They have only a slightly better concurrence to fact than two other common receptacles of unconscious projection, often populated with fantastic monsters—the Deep Blue Sea and the Edge of the Map.

Some months later, Greg Prichard was busy pursuing his research in the north of India when he came upon a cache of texts at a temple in Banaras. Among these many ancient texts, he unearthed an obscure—and probably unique—text handwritten on paper made from the fronds of a particular palm. It recounted a legend concerning a pair of temples in ancient India linked by a network of tunnels passing beneath a holy mountain. There was nothing in the text to indicate which temples the text was referring to, or even whether the events depicted, which were highly imaginative and seemed to be lending flesh to an abstract philosophic notion, were purely allegorical.

Certain internal references, coupled with the lack of external correlates, made it clear to him that although this text was of great antiquity, the writer of the text seemed to be putting to paper a legend that at the time of its writing was but a distant echo of a history that had already been all but forgotten, thus situating the events described, if they *were* actual events, in a past anterior to the obscure past in which the text itself was written.

Understanding the text was not easy; not only was the language archaic and difficult, parts of it were fragmentary. There were places where letters had been eaten by worms, pages that were entirely missing. Yet the history it told was so large that the author, of whom nothing is know, told it from varying perspectives. Therefore, if a particular event or story was missing from one account, it would be found in another. After much careful study and correlating of stories, he was able to put together the entire legend, which went something like this:

Once, long ago [and remember, this was written in a text of great antiquity], there was a holy mountain that rose from a vast plain. For untold *kalpas*, or great eons of time, the mountain had been known to have tremendous power and had served as a magnet for holy people. The presence of holy people attracted pilgrims, those searching out the company of sages. The singular nature of the mountain ensured its enduring power.

Over time, a princely state arose around this mountain, which acquired tremendous wealth, largely gained through the gifts lavished at the feet of the mountain's holy denizens. The wealth of the people was reflected in the ornate beauty of their temples, which they built at the base of their holy mountain. Over the course of time and through the reign of successive maharajas, the number of temples increased in both number and opulence as the town that grew up around them also acquired a wealth unrivalled in that part of India.

Wise to the danger disproportionate wealth can produce, the twenty-seventh maharaja in the line built and fortified a wall around the temple complex to protect the riches stored there from would-be marauders. By the reign of the thirty-first in the line, the amorphous danger of pillagers had solidified into a growing threat from a kingdom to the north that was gaining strength as a military force and was known for its brutal expansionist tendencies.

The maharaja, dressed incognito, went up the mountain to find the cave of a sage worthy of giving him advice. At each cave he revealed himself and the growing danger his people were in. He listened to what each had to say, but he didn't stop until he got to the cave of the one who was not only able to see the future, but knew how to positively affect the future by deeds. This, the maharaja knew, was wisdom, and he put into effect a secret construction program recommended by this sage to save his kingdom should it ever come under attack.

And so it came to pass some years later that warriors from the north swooped down on this princely state, a ripe cherry for the plucking. Everybody in the entire princely kingdom, even the yogis and sages who lived in caves upon the mountain, took refuge behind the fortified walls of the temple complex and helped man the gates.

Having only limited supplies and being a people shaped by the proximity of holy men and not themselves a warlike people, they didn't last long: three days by one account, two days by another. When it became clear that it wouldn't be long until their fortified gates were battered down and the marauders from the north had their way with the women, slaughtered the men, and took away all their riches, the maharaja revealed the great secret: a huge stone in the center of the main temple's floor, which was deceptively thin, was lifted to reveal the entrance to a tunnel that led to a natural network of caves and passages into which the entire population quickly passed.

The last act the maharaja himself made before disappearing into the tunnel was to pour a bottle of a very special potion that the sage had concocted into the well, which was the only source of water for the entire complex. It was a draught of forgetfulness powerful enough to make all those who drank from the well forget both where they came from and where they were going.

The king's system was so ingeniously designed that when the flat rock was put back into place covering the cave entrance from below there was no way to tell that it hadn't been lying there since the most distant mythical times.

A mere hour after they disappeared into the tunnel and put back the stone, their enemies smashed down the complex's three gates and swarmed into the temple complex, hot with the triple lusts of violence, rape, and plunder. But to their dumbfoundment, when they surged through the gates simultaneously in order to stun the people inside, there was no one there! They attempted to track them down to their hiding places but they were nowhere to be found. This simply could not be: an entire people missing! The walls had been surrounded. There was no way they could have escaped.

This unhinged quite a few of them, who ran from the place screaming, fearing black magic.

Others, of a more rational turn of mind, searched minutely, first for the hiding place and then for the route of escape. When there was no rational explanation for the disappearance of so many people, they too suspected supernatural causes, but benevolent ones, as if the gods had granted them a boon, as they realized the land they would take by force was suddenly theirs for the taking. Some ancient legends told them that this land was once theirs, and therefore their taking this land was justified; this now seemed confirmed as people slowly realized the temples, the town, the land, and everything on it had been abandoned and was theirs without a fight.

When they discovered the great storehouse of food, they cooked a sumptuous celebratory feast, for which, of course, they used the water from the well, which had been tainted with the potion of forgetfulness.

The next morning the entire marauding army from the north forgot why they were there. One man who had been a cowherd before he joined the invading force saw some cows untended, their udders bursting with milk. He simply herded them together and started milking them as if they were his own.

A man who worked metal came upon a metal workshop with the huge bellows and simply started fixing broken weapons, turning many of them into more practical farm implements. A man who tilled the earth saw the surrounding fields were in need of harvesting. Getting some scythes from the metal worker's new shop and gathering a workforce comprised of those who used to work the soil, he simply started harvesting. And thus everyone forgot from where they had come and the manner in which they had come, and simply took over the duties that were theirs before they set out on their adventure of conquest. In a very short time life went on as if there had never been a change of regime.

Meanwhile the former inhabitants, who had disappeared from the face of the earth by entering her bowels, had followed the tunnels made by their maharaja, which communicated with a huge natural network of caves and passages—which geologists would tell us were vent holes of the extinct volcano—and came out on the opposite side of the mountain where there was a similarly disguised rock set in the floor of a smaller temple. From there they were able to gather their strength and launch a successful surprise attack on their former home and win it back. Their enemy, retaining nothing of how they'd gotten there and that there was a people displaced who might very well one day return, were thoroughly unprepared.

Instead of the rape and pillage and murder that would have been meted out on them, they simply drove the invaders north, back to their own country. Forgetting they had come from the north and were themselves marauders, they felt their expulsion a great injustice and that they were being forced into exile.

The maharaja and his people were delighted to be back after their tremendous trials, so much so that the maharaja ordered a huge feast. Not really thinking, and then entirely forgetting, they used the water from the well for cooking and drinking. The water still contained enough of the draught of forgetfulness to be effective. By the very next morning everyone forgot their ordeal. The metal worker simply went to his shop to do his work as the farmer went to the fields to do his. The Maharaja once again ruled over his land and people, and even the holy men returned to their caves on the mountain to meditate and continue their dreams and contemplations. The draught in the well became diluted. For a while people forgot little things, like the names of distant relatives, but with time even this inconvenience disappeared.

Life in this princely state was quite as it was before. Since no one remembered the attack, or for that matter the tunnels, it was truly as if nothing had happened. As the text said, *Time returned to its origin.*

That is, until some generations later when the people to the north regained the power they had dissipated in their failed attack, and with tremendous self righteousness decided to swoop down on the mountain and its temple complex and retake the princely state, which their ancestors said was theirs and taken from them. When word of this reached the Maharaja—nobody could remember what number he was in the line—he went to one of the wisest of the holy men who lived in a deep cave on the mountain who told him that their only chance of survival was to locate a hidden network of tunnels he had seen in certain visionary states, which the maharaja did.

The rest, as they say, is history.

Events occurred exactly as they had before, down to the detail of the draught of forgetfulness given to the maharaja by the sage, the disappearance of an entire people, their return from behind the mountain and their triumphal retaking of the temple complex. This was followed by a celebratory feast in which they drank from the Well of Forgetfulness and lived on as if nothing had occurred.

The text went on to say that the entire cycle had recurred innumerable times through an unknown number of great ages, or *kalpas*, ever since Brahma first lay on the Cosmic Serpent and started dreaming time and the world into existence. It further stated that it would recur without end until the dream of life ceased in some unimaginably distant future, when all of existence is reabsorbed into the milky ocean of oneness from which it arose, and time ceases to exist. The text said—speaking, Greg felt, directly to him—that if an age comes in which people doubt the eternal recurrence of the great cycle, or think it a thing of the past or of legend, and forget the existence of the tunnels, it will only mean that the world was living through the cycle's long recurring interval marked by forgetfulness.

Had Greg read this text before he had gone to the mountain and encountered the thorn bushes—or thorn demons, as he'd been warned—if he hadn't had that frightful, yet illuminating night, he would have relished and found intellectually stimulating what this repetition of a cycle of history had to say about the ancient Indian cultural conception of time. He would have silently praised the text's long-diseased writer, whom he would have considered a master of the vanished poetic art of applying imagination to abstract thought in the name of storytelling, mirroring what Brahma himself does by spinning the underlying principles of existence into this world of vastly interlocking life stories. He would have interpreted it as a philosophic tale, an observation about the nature of time given flesh, in the form of a story without corollary in the 'real world.'

Greg traveled back to South India. He returned to the mountain. He went to the temple, and pretending to prostrate himself before the main altar he held his nose to a crack between a particularly large flat stone and the one next to it. With a flush of excitement he felt a rush of cold, dry air enter his lungs that smelled as old as time itself. In that draught of cold air he took in the tremendous sweep of time and history as it can be found nowhere else but in India, where all of recorded history is but a blink in the eye of Brahma, who lies on a multi-headed serpent floating on the milky ocean of being, dreaming this world into existence.

In the Den of the
Siberian Tiger

The hill town of Darjeeling, in India's eastern Himalayas, was built by the British in the early 19th century. It straddles a steep ridge of mountain running roughly north-south at 7,500 to 8,000 feet above sea level. The town is typically cold in winter and, because it is often unable to poke its head out from the cloud that seems perpetually to blanket it, it is damp.

One typically misty afternoon in winter, I went to the Darjeeling zoo to see the Siberian tigers. In 1960, no doubt as a gesture to cement friendly relations, Nikita Khrushchev gave this zoo two Siberian tigers. I'd never been to the zoo and I usually don't like going, but I wanted to see their progeny. Siberian Tigers are the largest of the cats, and are considered the planet's most powerful hunters.

Just how strong they were, even before seeing one of them, was clear in the make of their enclosures, which were thicker and higher than any at the zoo. Everything was outsized, the bars almost unreasonably thick, the fence around their runs a mesh of steel, the moats deep, the reinforced concrete bunkers looking fit for an aerial bombardment. The fenced runs mounted a hillside, long strips of land side by side. And inside each the ground was well worn with trails the tigers pound while pacing endlessly the confines of their captivity.

As I came closer, I saw at the bottom of the first run a lone gold- and black-striped cat. It was pacing a perfect figure eight, tracing and retracing its steps in the dusty earth and had done so so endlessly that it had packed a trail. Its gait was so smooth, its huge padded feet conducting its tremendous weight so effortlessly, that it was as if its body floated above the ground tracing and retracing its endless loop. Grace confined.

The bunker was comprised of separate thick-walled cells. Each had a guillotine door opening to its run. These doors, each a thick plate of iron raised and lowered with cables and pulleys, were manipulated from the outside with huge levers and wires like the ones used on train track switches. Siberian tigers are solitary beasts and cannot all be put out together. Their tremendous might—and, I might say, noble, if buried, longing for freedom—was evinced in the thickness of all that confined them.

Then from within the bunker I heard another of the Siberian tigers. It let out a roar, like none I could have imagined, haunting in its resonate hollow despair. I came closer and it let out another roar. It came from a waist-high door of thick metal bars deeply pitted with rust and green with the mold of the damp Darjeeling winter. The massive walls, built to withstand the might of these Siberian giants, sweated with moist, pungent air, heavy with the odor of tiger. As I approached the door and crouched down to look within, holding my nose against the fetid stench of urea and damp, animal-laden air, the beast bellowed yet again.

It took some moments for my eyes to adjust to the darkness within that cell, to see the low wooden platform, the stone basin for water. The tiger's den had the ascetic feel of a holy man's cave. And as my eyes accustomed to the darkness, I saw the tiger's head. I could just make out its front shoulders. The rest of the beast lay in profound darkness. Its head was immense, its mouth, one a trainer could truly put his head in. Never had I seen a cat so large as that grand patriarch in its concrete lair. The powerful stench stung my nostrils. I breathed through the sleeve of my thick woolen sweater. The tiger lifted its head, opened its mouth, and roared. The ground beneath my feet shook.

Someone approached me from behind. It was the tiger's keeper, a barefoot Nepali man holding in both hands a large metal bowl of water. I moved aside from where I had been squatting. He put the bowl on the ground and took from his pocket a large key, which he used to unlock the padlock on the door. Everything about the door was outsized, built to withstand the full force of the Siberian tiger.

He slid back the bolt and pushed open the door. Then he lifted the bowl of water and crawled through the door into the tiger's den. He walked stooping, his head bent to the side to accommodate the cell's low ceiling, to where the tiger lay. It took a moment for me to comprehend fully that the door was open and nothing separated me from this Siberian patriarch. At first I thought it an illusion, like a play of mirrors that makes a distant object look within reach. But it was no illusion. Nothing stood between me and the tiger. It would take but a single swipe of the tiger's paw for it to overcome its keeper and be free. As I realized the full reality of this, a feeling of vertigo came over me, as if suddenly I found myself on the edge of a huge gaping precipice. Adrenaline flushed to the tips of my fingers. The instinct arose to flee. But the keeper's fearlessness, his deep concentration and calm, stopped me.

As if he were bowing before a god deep in a cave temple, the keeper lowered the bowl to the tiger's mouth. The tiger opened its maw and lapped water with its huge tongue. When the bowl was empty the man picked up the bowl, turned his back on the tiger, and left the cell, locking it behind him.

I squatted again by the door to the tiger's cell. The tiger lifted its head and roared. It struggled to get to its feet— but it couldn't do it, its movements jerky and uncoordinated. Rolling its head from side to side, it wailed, the stones resounding with its force. I could see now the flaccid muscles of this once- majestic beast. I sat by that door, the stench of the dying giant clinging to me and penetrating my clothes, until the sun was setting and the zoo closed.

I returned the next day, listening and peering into the darkness. Strangely, I felt honored to be the sole witness of the end of this majestic beast's life. Every breath was for it an attempted roar—as if to rile against its fate—but all it could muster was a moan; and its body shuddered with each breath. It was lying with its head pressed in the very corner of its cell, against concrete on one side and the pitted, molding, rusted iron bars on the other. Occasionally it tried to get up, but its legs could not coordinate and every attempt ended in an angry roar followed by a moan of despair. It was in this corner, with his head against the bars, that it would die. Never had I seen a cat so huge as this great old giant. To see what must once have been of such majesty and power reduced to a sack of miserable flesh was tremendous.

When I returned the next day, the cell was empty. The keeper told me he had died overnight. They had already brought his corpse to the jungle and cremated it.

THE TOWER OF DARAMDIN

The Land Where Hidden Treasures Rise: that is the name the Lepchas—the aboriginal people of Darjeeling and Sikkim tucked away in India's eastern Himalayas—call their land. I learned this from Dugay Lepcha, the head of the Lepcha Cultural Association. I had been particularly interested in learning about the Lepchas because there was something about them to this day that seemed innocent, prior to the corruption that has overtaken the Hills with the successive waves of immigrants into what was once their domain.

Dugay lives in Darjeeling town, just below the zoo and behind Mama's Tea Stall, down a short flight of stairs, around the back with his wife and mother-in-law in an apartment of tiny rooms off a low hallway.

Dugay and I hit it off immediately. His warm and open face, gentleness of spirit, and welcoming nature made me feel immediately at home. I sat on a couch and Dugay sat cross-legged on a wide cushioned platform that would be made into his bed at night.

"Darjeeling and Sikkim were once one land," he said. "In my language, we call this land *Mayel Lyang*. That means hidden land, a land of refuge. We also call it *Mayel Maluk Lyang*; that means the land in which the hidden treasure will rise. We have many legends, many stories, ancient stories, stories older than your Bible, things for which we hold the key. We are the children of the sacred mountain Kanchenjunga. Our legends say we were created from the pristine snows of her slopes. We do not believe in reincarnation like the Buddhists. We come from the mountain, we live on her slopes, and when we die, we return to the mountain. In our own language, we call ourselves the *Mutanchi Rongkup*.

That means 'mothers beloved ones.' The name 'Lepcha' is not our word. It comes from a Nepali word, *Lapca*, meaning 'nonsense talkers.' When the Nepalis came they couldn't understand us, so they thought we spoke nonsense. They had no idea the Lepcha language is far older than theirs. They didn't know the Lepcha language is older than your English, older than Hebrew, Latin, or even Sanskrit."

"I didn't know it either," I said. "But how's it possible?"

"Not many know this," Dugay said in a voice at once low and quivering with intensity, as if intent on bestowing a great secret. He leaned toward me. "Ours was the first language spoken on earth."

He waited for his words to fully register.

"And we're not the only ones who have known this. You must have heard of Colonel G. B. Mainwaring, who wrote the first Lepcha grammar and dictionary in the 1870s."

I hadn't.

"When he died he was working on a book proving Lepcha is at the root of all languages. He had discovered that words in many languages, even in English, are similar to Lepcha words and have their root there."

"Who was this Colonel Mainwaring?" I asked.

"He was a British officer with the Bengal Staff Corps based in Calcutta. His duties brought him into contact with the Lepchas. He became fascinated with them and entered their world. He even married a Lepcha, a *mun*, which is what we call our priestesses. He delved deeply into our hidden past. A few other Westerners have studied the Lepchas, but they haven't gone from place to place, to the villages. They just read the books written by other researchers and they write new books. And the lies get passed on. Mainwaring became half a Lepcha himself. He understood our world. To learn about the Lepchas you cannot learn it from books. You cannot learn it from towns or libraries. To learn about the Lepchas, you must go to the villages.

"If you like, one day I will take you. We can travel to some Lepcha villages. We will have to walk far. Up the side of a mountain. Then you can see our culture. Lepcha people are very peace loving. They live far from town, on the hilltop and at the bottom of the hill. The Lepcha nature is like that. They don't like it very crowded—they prefer it 'far from the madding crowd.'

"In most of our villages there is still no electrification. No roads, no drinking water. In some villages, they fetch water in what we call a *daram*, a wide section of bamboo, which they strap to their backs. Sometimes they have to walk three hours to bring water to their village. And they will run away if they see a stranger. That is how the Britishers took our land.

"All of Sikkim and what is now the Darjeeling Hills used to be under the Sikkimese king. When the Nepalis invaded in the early 1800s the British helped the king and drove the Nepalis off the land. In thanks, though the king was basically forced into it, the British got the southern half of the kingdom, beginning with the ridge upon which Darjeeling Town now sits. This was in 1835, and at that time Darjeeling was virgin forest. And what do you think the Britishers did once they won and got the land?"

He looked intently at me, his hand raised in a quizzical gesture. My look told him I hadn't a clue.

"They brought the Nepalis they had just fought off the land back in as workers to clear-cut the forests; they burnt it to the ground. The Lepchas didn't put up a fight. We just moved to more remote areas.

"In the Lepcha language there is no word for war. We didn't even have the concept. We were a peaceful people, living with nature. We were nature worshippers, worshipping mountains, rivers, and trees. Everything that gave us life we gave thanks to. The trees nourished us, they gave us shade. We used their wood for our houses. From their bark we made rope. We ate their nuts. In their thickets lived the animals we hunted. In the forest and by the stream were all the medicinal herbs for every ailment. The Lepchas are tremendous botanists. We know every plant, which are safe to eat, which not. It was the forest that gave us life. The river gave us water, gave us fish. At that time there was no greed, no enemy. No! Everything we needed, we got from Mother Nature. We had nothing to worry about at that time. It was a very beautiful time.

"And there was no hierarchy, even in our religion. We had the *boomthing* and the *mun*, our priests and priestesses, who performed rituals and did sacrifices, who were intermediaries between our world and the spirit world, the world of our ancestors. But there was no hierarchy of *boomthing* or *mun*. Not like with the Tibetan lamas."

In the corner of the room was a shrine with images that were clearly Buddhist. "But you are a Buddhist?"

"I follow both. I follow the lamas and I follow our old nature worship, the *boomthing* and *mun*. That is how most Lepchas are now. Although some are Christian. Christian Lepchas don't follow the *boomthing*. Christianity doesn't allow it. Christianity is more exclusive. One god, and all of that. Christian Lepchas know less of the old traditions."

"How did the Lepchas convert to these religions?" I asked.

"Christianity they got from the Britishers. But long before that the Bhutias came. *Bhutia* is another name for Tibetan. Way back, in the 1600s, the Tibetans were fighting amongst themselves and some fled south over the high passes into Sikkim. They founded a kingdom here. It was based on their Tibetan culture. That's how the kingdom of Sikkim was founded. And it was larger than Sikkim is now, including what is now Sikkim and the Darjeeling Hills, as well as parts of what are now eastern Nepal and western Bhutan. They brought with them Buddhism, and they converted us. Many Lepchas started practicing both Buddhism and the older nature worship. The Buddhists took our ancient books, written in our own script, and they burnt them so we would lose our old beliefs—so we would become Buddhist.

"There are other people from Tibet here now. They are refugees, those that fled the Chinese invasion of Tibet in 1959. The earlier ones, the Bhutias, founded a dynasty of rulers in the 1600s. They were called the *chogyals*, or kings. During this time most Lepchas began practicing both nature worship and Buddhism. From the founding of the *chogyals* until the British came, Mayel Lyang was basically a vassal state of

Tibet. That is why to this day the Chinese, who consider Tibet part of China, also consider Sikkim to be a part of China. In 1962 they even fought a war over this, the Indo-Chinese war. They fought on the high passes to Tibet.

"Our land was once the Garden of Eden. Lepcha was the language of Eden. We never left. The garden got cut in two, or three, or four—by outsiders. Paradise with a fence down the middle is no longer Paradise. Isn't that so?"

Dugay's wife came in with tea and a plate of cookies. She set it before us and left the room.

Dugay continued: "The real troubles for the Lepchas came with the British. We were children of nature. Gentle people. Traditional Lepcha houses are constructed with five huge tree trunks upon which the rest of the house is built. Five huge uprights, you see—one in each corner and one in the middle. But we don't dig holes and put these five tree trunks into the ground. That would be to hurt the earth, which is our mother. We place the five tree trunks on big flat stones. Our houses rest on these flat stones. They rest on the earth; they are not attached. This is good for when an earthquake comes. The houses are not tied into the earth, in which case they would be broken up. Rather they can glide and skate on the flat stones and nothing happens to them. Recently some Japanese scientists came to study our traditional way of building and they brought the idea back to Japan, where they have many earthquakes. They are now building houses on the same principle. The world has a lot to learn from the Lepchas.

"We were a gentle people, not wanting even to dig into the earth. And then the British came. They wanted Darjeeling for a sanitarium for all the Britishers who lived in Calcutta and got sick there in the hot climate. The climate of Darjeeling was perfect for their needs. So they built the town and with time they clear-cut the forests in all the mountains and they burnt them too."

Dugay got an ironic smile. "They did it all for this," and he lifted his cup and took a sip of tea. "Once they established their sanitarium here they discovered the climate was also perfect for tea. That is when they invited back all the Nepalis

LEPCHA HOUSE FOUNDATION:
TREE TRUNK RESTING ON FLAT STONE

they had just routed by war. They invited them to clear the forests and work the tea. Now Darjeeling tea is famous the world over—and the majority of people in Darjeeling are Nepalis. We Lepchas are now a minority in our own land."

"Why didn't they employ the Lepchas?" I asked.

"It wasn't in our nature. Why would we work for others when we could get everything we needed from nature? We disappeared into the shadows; whenever someone moved in on our land, we simply moved to where we'd be left alone.

"It's because the Lepchas are a peace-loving people that we don't have our own country. That's the course of history, at least in Darjeeling.

"It's not unusual, even today, for a stranger to enter a Lepcha village and think it is abandoned. Sometimes even if *I* go to a remote village I have to call out to them in Lepcha, 'No, no, no—come back, I will not hurt you.' It is still like that. In many of the villages far flung from town they don't know Nepali, they don't know English. They only speak Lepcha. A lot of villages are like that. They haven't seen Kalimpong Town, they haven't seen Darjeeling. They've only heard the names. When you come with me you'll see."

Dugay's wife came in to tell him there was someone at the door. He stood on his bed and took down a book from a high shelf. He blew the dust off it and handed it to me.

"This is the grammar of the Lepcha language written by Colonel Mainwaring. He opened the front cover. "It was first published in 1876. Have a look, I will be right back." Dugay Lepcha sprung off his bed and left the room.

I flipped through the introduction, and there I found statements echoing what Dugay had said about Lepcha being of tremendous antiquity, the language, as he had put it, spoken in the Garden of Eden. I felt as if I had stumbled upon one of those mysteries that the land was named for: *Mayel Maluk Lyang*, the Land in which Hidden Treasures Rise.

Dugay's exaggerated assertions about his dying culture could easily be dismissed. What did he know of the study of linguistics? But here I was, holding a scholarly tome written by a British colonel, perhaps the only Westerner of his time to delve deeply into this vanishing culture. This is an obscure corner of this earth, tucked away in the vastness of the Himalayas. Its very obscurity could easily hide tremendous secrets. The vastness of the landscape begged it. Could it be that these simple, peaceful people held a tremendous jewel for humanity, the very key to all languages, lying in obscurity since the 1870s? Or was the colonel simply a mad Britisher who'd gone native?

Here is some of what the colonel wrote:

> The language is...unquestionably far anterior to the Hebrew or Sanskrit. It is preeminently an *Ursprache*, being probably, and I think, I may, without fear of misrepresentation, state it to be, the oldest language extant. It is a most comprehensive and beautiful one; and regarded alone, as a prolific source of the derivations and etyma of words, it

is invaluable to the philological world. It however
recommends itself to us on higher grounds; it pos-
sesses and plainly evinces the principle and mo-
tive on which all language is constructed. But, like
everything really good in this world, it has been
despised and rejected. To allow the Lepcha race,
and the language to die out would indeed be most
barbarous, and inexpressibly sad.

... In the structure of the Lepcha language, I
have discovered the system on which, I consider,
all language is based. By an exegesis which I have,
in part prepared, (combined with a diagram showing the rudimental powers of letters), the roots and
true significations of all words in all languages,
are, at once, rendered apparent.

Dugay returned.

I hardly looked up from the book.

"Ah, you are enjoying Mainwaring's book?" he asked.

"Very much," I exclaimed. "This is tremendous. But tell
me, where did the Lepchas come from? Where did they live
before coming to *Mayel Lyang*?"

"Scholars have been debating that since the outside world
first made contact with us. They have their theories. Some
have written their books saying we migrated from the east,
from the hill tribes of Assam. Some say we came from the
south. Some say we were originally a tribe that came from
the east, from Nepal. And some say we came from the north,
that we are descended from the Mongolians or Tibetans.
Some have even said we are the lost tribe of Israel. There
is even a story that we descended from three warriors that
stayed behind when Alexander the Great marched east and
somehow came to these mountains.

"I'll tell you something: they are all wrong. Long ago
there was a great civilization, and after that there was a
disaster. Everything vanished and new generations came,
new creations. The Lepchas are the last vestige of that
ancient civilization. In that time—I believe it's true, isn't

it—in Europe they used to walk naked, they wore animal skins. While you Europeans were walking naked, we Lepchas were civilized."

He saw the disbelief on my face. Disbelief alloyed with a healthy dose of wonder.

"Long ago there was a flood. It ended a whole epoch of human civilization. The only to escape were a group of Lepchas, who went atop the sacred Tendong Hill, that's just north of here in Sikkim. That is why our language is the root of all, why our culture is the oldest. The flood lasted for forty days. I know what you think, that it sounds just like the flood from the Bible. That's because they stole it! The truth of the matter is that the Lepcha story is older than that of your Bible. It is the original. The Bible story comes from the Lepcha. You really must go there, to Tendong Hill. It is a very sacred place, and now it's a nature preserve. There are many caves there; holy men live in the caves. Every year we Lepchas have a big festival there to celebrate the water's receding. All during the monsoon, people pray to the mountain that the waters will not rise so high again."

"What makes you think the Lepcha story is older than the Biblical flood?" I asked.

"That's not the only story we have that was put into the Bible," he said, bolstering his story by telling another. "In ancient times, the Lepchas went to a place called Daramdin, which is in southwestern Sikkim. As you will see, the story is similar in every respect to your Tower of Babel.

"Once, long ago, a band of Lepcha gathered at Daramdin to build a tower to Heaven. They used fired clay pots to build their tower, and the tower became so high that the people at the top and the people at the bottom could no longer understand each other. The tower reached so close to Heaven that the people at the top only needed a pole with a hook on it to actually grab onto Heaven. So they called down, "Send up a hook," a message that was relayed by shouting from person to person down the tower. But the people at the bottom couldn't understand. "What?" they yelled back. That 'What?'

was relayed up and up and up the tower till the people at the top again yelled down, "Send up a hook!" Again, the people at the bottom could not understand. This shouting up and down the tower continued for some time until the people at the bottom thought they understood. What they heard was, 'Smash the tower.' Unfortunately, the two sentences are very similar in the ancient Lepcha language. So they did. They smashed the tower and the whole thing came crashing down, killing everyone on it. The surviving Lepchas, those that had been on the ground, scattered, and no one knows what became of them."

Disbelief must have been written on my face.

"If you don't believe me, you can go there and see for yourself," he said mater-of-factly.

"What?"

"Although this happened long ago—thousands of years ago, if the truth be known—if you go to Daramdin you can still find pieces of the broken pottery they used to make the tower to Heaven. They are still coming out of the ground. There are so many always surfacing that the farmers of Daramdin find it difficult to plow their fields. You really *must* go to Daramdin. If you go to Daramdin, I tell you: you will find pieces of the ancient Lepcha's tower to Heaven!"

"Have you been there?"

"Of course," he said, "many times. I've seen this with my own eyes."

This was just the sort of place to fire my imagination, a place on this earth that wasn't of it. Finding a piece of the Lepchas' tower to Heaven would be like finding a piece of a unicorn's horn. Or a feather on the floor the morning after dreaming of an angel.

Some time later, I crossed the border north to Sikkim. I was on a walking tour, walking from village to village when I recalled Dugay Lepcha and the Lepcha Tower to Heaven.

Around a tight bend in the road an elderly man was walking in the opposite direction. A walking stick made of bamboo in his right hand aided his purposeful stride. He stopped a few paces in front of me and a smile lighted on his face. Resting both hands on the top of his length of bamboo he asked me where I was going on such a lonely road.

I asked him if he knew of a place called Daramdin.

"Of course," he said. "The Lepchas, my distant ancestors, built their tower to Heaven there."

"Have you been to Daramdin?"

"Not in twenty years," he said. "It is a big flat area of land—perhaps the only one in Sikkim!" He burst out laughing.

"Is it true," I asked, "that if you go there, you can still find pieces of the tower?"

"And why not?" he said. "A tower that high, falling down, what do you think would happen with all those broken pots? Even after who knows how many years—thousands, I suppose—where would they go? I saw them with my own eyes. The pots they used, some of them, were quite large. I guess those were at the bottom."

Then he looked at me with a peculiar look. "You never told me," he said, "where are you going?"

"Daramdin," I said confidently.

"How will you get there?" he asked. "Daramdin is very remote, tucked away in rough mountains towards Nepal. The road is very difficult."

"Am I headed in the right direction?"

"Quite certainly," he said.

"Then you tell me."

He smiled and gave me directions, which would take days to follow if I went on foot, but he explained how at a certain crossroads I could catch a ride on a public jeep that would take me to Sombaria, a market town right next to Daramdin. Dugay Lepcha had given me the name of a friend of his who lives in Sombaria whom I could stay with and who knows the history and could take me to the site of the tower.

I caught a ride for a short way with a local man in a beat-up old truck. He, too, had been to Daramdin, about six or eight years earlier, and he said there were so many pieces of pottery there that when they made a new road nearby, they used them for pavement.

I walked more, caught another ride or two, and everybody had heard of the tower and some had been there and seen with their own eyes the ancient remains. I got to the crossroads that the old man with the cane mentioned. And there I waited until a share jeep came along and stopped for me. It was going to Sombaria, and I jumped in. Share jeeps in Sikkim are like taxis. Although one pays for a seat, one usually gets just enough space to plant half of one's ass; if one is lucky one also gets a piece of reinforcing rod that holds up the canvas canopy to hold on to.

Sometimes the jeeps are overloaded with sacks of rice or potatoes lashed to the roof, which causes them to lean dangerously—as if in response to a magnetic force—every time a steep abyss presents itself on the side of the road, threatening to set the whole rattling mess of steel and rubber and human beings tumbling to a certain end.

This jeep had a consignment of watermelons from one of the passengers' gardens lashed to the roof racks, one of which bounced off when the vehicle hit a particularly large pothole and smashed on the receding pavement. This misfortune occasioned a little celebration on the side of the road as we enjoyed the broken bounty of his harvest.

The small market town of Sombaria, set in steep-sloped and rugged mountains, looked like the set for a Western movie with its wood slat houses, dusty main road, and even something that looked like a saloon with swinging wooden half doors right next to where the jeep dropped me. Feeling literally shaken, rattled, and as if I'd been rolled over by the long journey, I stepped into the wood-slat restaurant for a cup of tea to rest before finding Dugay's friend. I nodded my hello to two middle-aged village women at the next table. They were wearing Tibetan dress and had a dangerous air about them, boisterous with drink and practically falling off their chairs. They started rustling up the proprietress to get a third glass so I could drink brandy with them. It was like walking into a saloon scene of a Western movie, one that probably ends with their husbands swaggering in through the swinging half doors. Instead of guns they'd be brandishing *kukris*, the local sword that is used for just about everything. I ordered a tea, drank it quickly, then found a boy who knew where to find Dugay's friend.

I followed the boy through some alleys up the slope above the bazaar. We came to a low building full of people. They were singing hymns. I looked inside. It was a Christian church. I turned around and the boy was gone. There were some kids hanging about outside and I asked them where I could find Dugay's friend. One of them, eager to use his English and be helpful, led me to his house.

I was brought to a sitting room while tea was prepared. Various women and children flashed their faces at the door like phantoms, just to catch a glimpse of me. I learned from a plaque on the wall that Dugay's friend was the head of the Lepcha Cultural Association for West Sikkim. The rest of the walls were taken up with posters of little blond girls wearing formal party dresses that looked out of 18th century England with saccharine sayings such as, "You Know How to Bring a Smile to My Face." Or, "Love You. Really Do." Or, "If You Care for Someone, Show it." In one, a five-year-old blond girl, red powder on her cheeks, false eyelashes adorning her dark blue eyes and dressed for a formal garden party was standing next to an equally dapper little blond boy in a bowler hat and suspenders. The photo was slightly blurred for romantic effect. The two, who were only a few years out of diapers, were holding hands. "Life Smiles When We Are Together," the caption read.

These posters—which I'd seen before, both for sale in the market and in people's homes, but never in such concentration—always gave me an uneasy feeling. Maybe it was the implicit sexuality of these little girls made up to look like someone's ideal of femininity. Maybe it was that these posters sold because of an ideal of beauty in light-skinned little blond girls in a land of dark-skinned, dark-haired people. It always made my mind turn to pedophiles and Barbie dolls.

Tea was brought, and I was left alone to drink it. Then the boy who'd brought me there ran in, sweating and out of breath. With a huge smile on his face, he explained that Dugay's friend was in a hospital in Gangtok with an ulcer. "I just ran home to see my father," he told me. "It will be difficult for you to stay here. Our house is bigger and my father speaks English. He's a Christian preacher. You can stay with us!"

As we walked out of the village towards his family's house along the ridge, I was curious what this boy knew of the story of the ancient tower. So I asked him if he had ever heard of it. He had, and pointed down the slope to a flat area of fields. It was the only flat piece of land of any size I'd ever seen in Sikkim.

THE PLAIN OF DARAMDIN

"It was built right down there on those fields," he said, "and it rose higher than we are here. They tried to reach the sky."

On three sides of this 'plain' the land dropped off a couple hundred feet almost vertically to a sharp bend in a river. It was easy to imagine a tower being built there as a man-made continuation of what was in effect a naturally truncated tower. Spectacular wooded mountains rose behind. It did something to me to be so close to the site of this mysterious tower, built by this boy's ancestors in a remote past. The landscape practically called for a tower to be built. At one time this remote corner of Sikkim must have been the center of a culture whose greatness was now almost lost without a trace. Only the broken pieces of pottery, remains of the fallen tower scattered across the Plain of Daramdin, attest to these people who once aspired to reach Heaven. As it says in the Bible of the builders of the Tower of Babel, "from there the Lord scattered them over the face of the whole earth."

"If I go down there tomorrow," I asked my little guide, "could you tell me where to find pieces of the tower? Are they difficult to find?"

"It used to be easier," he said. "Now maybe you have to pay some boys to help you." It seemed he was hoping to capitalize on my presence. For all I knew, it was a cottage industry among local children.

We arrived at his family's house, which was a little larger and more prosperous looking than its neighbors. I was led into a sitting room with couches and coffee tables and—of course—posters on the walls. Apart from the usual posters of young blond girls there was also a poster for the First Evangelical Church Association of India. In its center was a map of Sikkim. This was superimposed on what looked like the famous flag raising by American troops in Iwo Jima; but instead of the Stars and Stripes, the flag that was so heroically being raised was of Jesus and the Crown of Thorns. Sikkim itself had a large black cross in it with arrows pointing from it to each of its neighbors—Nepal, India, Bhutan, Tibet, and China—as if the mission of the Sikkimese Evangelical Church was to colonize the entirety of Asia.

His father was becoming successful in converting people in the next village over, where he had just opened his own church. He spoke English fluently and had received an education.

I was unsure what he might think about the tower since, as Dugay told me, Buddhism is more syncretic and less exclusive, and Christian Lepchas are less inclined than the Buddhists to know the old Lepcha stories.

Far from shunning the story, he embraced it. Since he was versed in the Bible, he described the striking resemblance between the Lepcha tower and the Tower of the Bible. In Daramdin the tower was made from fired pots, in Babel, from baked bricks. In both, the builders became unable to understand each other's language; and in both, while the builders would have liked to make a name for themselves, reach the very heavens, and leave a monument behind for all times, they were defeated and lost to obscurity. He explained that no one knows what became of those Lepchas who built the tower.

Then I asked him the question that was really the purpose of my being there, concerning my Holy Grail: "Can you tell me where to go so I can find pieces of the tower?"

"It's not so easy now," he said, "in fact—it is quite impossible. It was possible in my grandfather's time. The old people still speak of it; but now it is difficult. Sometimes, during monsoon, pieces wash out of the riverbank."

While we were speaking, two old men had come in to look at the foreigner who had come to their village. They sat cross-legged on the floor. I asked whether either of them had a piece of the tower. Surely such relics, if they could no longer be easily found, would be handed down through the generations. They shook their heads. It seemed nobody in the entire village had a piece.

Like the morning mist before the sun, all those pieces of the tower large and small, disturbing the plowing of fields, in such abundance as to be used to pave roads, dissolved without a trace upon my arrival. All the stories people told me, from Dugay on down, were just that: stories. Dugay would hear from me!

The unicorn horn of my quest would remain beyond reach.

Later I found out that the church I had been brought to when I arrived was the first Christian church in Sikkim, founded by Finnish missionaries who came from Darjeeling sometime in the 1800s. Was this just coincidence? Did the missionaries hear of the tower and link it to the biblical Tower? Did they invent the whole thing?

The next day I went down to Daramdin and found my way onto the plain, which was excellent farm land. There were channels for water between the cultivated fields, margins of tall grasses, and houses set between the fields. I inquired for the site of the tower and was led there by some young men to a plaque that had been laid there a year before. It explained that it was the future sight of a Lepcha museum. The boys further explained that they were also going to build a little mock tower out of clay pots. It was all part of a government economic development project to turn Daramdin, considered a backward area, into a tourist attraction.

ALSO BY THOMAS K. SHOR

A STEP AWAY FROM PARADISE:
The True Story of a Tibetan Lama's Journey
to a Land of Immortality
(also available AudioBook
and Russian & Chinese Translations)

THE BABA DOWNSTAIRS:
The Life Story of a Misfit Indian Saint

INTO THE HANDS OF THE UNKNOWN:
an Indian Sojourn with a Harvard Renunciant

THE MONK AND THE SLY CHICKPEA:
Travels on Corfu

THE MASTER DIRECTOR:
A Journey through Politics, Doubt and Devotion
with a Himalayan Master

LEOPARD IN THE CITY:
An Urban Fable

GANGES LAMENT:
Black and White Photographic Portraits
from the Sacred Indian City of Varanasi

SCULPTURE GARDEN OF THE GODS:
Animated Landscape Photography from
the Greek Island of Ikaria
(also available in English/Greek Edition)

About the Author

Writer and photographer Thomas K. Shor was born in Boston, USA, and studied comparative religion and literature in Vermont.

With an ear for unusual stories, the fortune to attract them, and an eye for detail, he has traveled the planet's mountainous realms—from the Mayan Highlands of southern Mexico in the midst of insurrection to the mountains of Greece, and more recently, to the Indian Himalayas—to collect, illustrate, and write stories with a uniquely personal character, often having the flavour of fable.

Shor has lectured widely on his writings and has had solo exhibits of his photographs in Europe and India. He can often be found in the most obscure locales, immersed in a compelling story touching upon fundamental human themes.

Visit him at:

www.ThomasShor.com